ALSO BY PAT HUGHES

Guerrilla Season

THE BREAKER BOYS

The Breaker Boys

PAT HUGHES

Farrar Straus Giroux / New York

Distributed in Canada by Douglas & McIntyre Ltd.
Printed in the United States of America
Designed by Nancy Goldenberg
First edition, 2004
3   5   7   9   10   8   6   4   2
www.fsgkidsbooks.com

Library of Congress Cataloging-in-Publication Data
Hughes, Pat (Patrice Raccio)
  The breaker boys / Pat Hughes.—1st ed.
    p.   cm.
  Summary: In 1897, Nate Tanner, the hot-tempered twelve-year-old son of a
wealthy Pennsylvania mine owner, goes against his father's wishes by befriending some
of the boys who work in the mines and gets caught up in a disastrous clash between
mine workers and the law.
  ISBN 0-374-30956-6
  [1. Coal miners—Fiction.   2. Coal mines and mining—Fiction.
3. Immigrants—Fiction.   4. Labor movement—Fiction.   5. Fathers and sons—
Fiction.   6. Stepfamilies—Fiction.   7. Pennsylvania—History—1865– —Fiction.]
  I. Title.

PZ7.H87374Br 2004
[Fic]—dc22   2003049433

For my sons, Tristan and Jesse, in the hope that they will accept no simplistic versions of history, but instead always ask questions, seek answers—and ponder the possibilities

THE BREAKER BOYS

1

"WATCH IT, Tanner!"

"Yeah, imbecile, quit pushing!"

Somebody thumped Nate's head as he edged between the lines of boys on the stairs. No time to retaliate, or even turn around. He slammed through the school door, dashed across the quadrangle, and took the dormitory steps three at a time.

In his fourth-floor room, he sifted through the papers and books scattered across his desk, mumbling, "Where is it, stupid book, where is it?" When his fingers closed on the Latin grammar, he was off again—but not fast enough.

The corridor was empty, every classroom door closed. Now he would surely have trouble. His steps echoed; he slowed to a walk. Fletcher had been badgering him for months, and Nate was sick of fighting it. All heads turned as he entered.

Fletcher gave him a got-you grin. "Well, Mr. *Tan*ner. How *good* of you to grace us with your presence. Why, you're all out of breath, dear boy! Anything I can get you? Cold drink, perhaps?"

Around the room, snickers ticked like falling dominoes.

Nate held up his book. "I had to—"

"Yes, yes, what's today's excuse?" Fletcher said wearily.

"I forgot my book."

Fletcher stretched out his arm. "Well, then, hand over your pass."

"I don't have one. I couldn't find a monitor."

"I *see.*" Fletcher paced, as if ruminating, then addressed the class: "Perhaps Mr. Tanner is of the opinion that because his family owns collieries, he needn't adhere to the rules as ordinary boys do."

More laughter. No surprise. Among all the boys, Nate didn't have a single friend.

"After all, *he'll* have charge of thousands of Pennsylvania coal miners soon enough, whether or not he is prompt to Latin class."

"I don't—"

Fletcher whirled. *"Silence!"* Striding back, he wagged his bony yellow finger under Nate's nose; the tobacco odor was nauseating. "You are an arrogant little boy, Tanner," Fletcher said, eyeing him with disgust. "You've wasted no opportunity to express your contempt for this school and everyone in it." He fumbled in his desk drawer, withdrawing a paddle. "And you arrive late again, with this lie about your book—"

"It's the truth!"

"Quiet!" Fletcher thwacked the desktop; the class jolted. "Step up!" Fletcher commanded.

Nate's anger blinded him with a white-hot light. He flung the grammar to the floor. "I won't," he said, teeth clenched. "I won't be thrashed by a lunatic, and if you—"

"Tanner!" Fletcher screamed, his neck veins bulging.

"If you try it, I'll make you sorry."

The boys gasped.

As Nate headed for the door, Fletcher grabbed hold of his sleeve. "Let go!" Nate pulled roughly away. Fletcher stumbled. Nate looked back to track Fletcher's progress and tripped over the wooden stand that held the Latin-English dictionary.

The boys laughed. Humiliated, Nate upended the stand. As it crashed, the heavy dictionary splayed open in front of Fletcher's advancing feet.

Nate ran.

"*Tanner!*" Fletcher yelled.

All along the corridor, curious teachers opened their doors. Nate dodged a hand that snatched at him. He careered down the stairs, across the quad, and off the school grounds.

2

ALONE OUTSIDE HAZLETON STATION, Nate sat on his trunk. He'd been waiting half an hour, watching the sun dip behind a dark and distant coal breaker. With each minute he grew more certain: no one would come.

He fished the telegram from his pocket and looked at it again.

DATED: HAZLETON, PENN.

TO: NATHAN TANNER   6/18 1897

TAKE NOON TRAIN TUESDAY 22ND. TICKET IN YOUR
NAME AT STATION.

No "Pa" at the end, and certainly no "love." Nate knew Pa wouldn't even listen to his side. At school, at home, everything was always his fault.

He crumpled the telegram and tossed it aside. His suit was too hot for June, and he was thirsty and very hungry. Should he get a porter to help with the trunk, and take the trolley home? Or ask to use the telephone? No. If he telephoned, they might think he cared. And if he turned up on his own, they might think he was anxious to get there.

Nate lifted his eyes as horses drew near.

"Natey! Hi!" Tory sang out. When the gleaming black brougham stopped, his older sister leaped out. "Sorry we're late—a trolley broke down right in front of us!" Nate stood and let her hug him tight. She stepped back to appraise him, her blue eyes sparkling. "Did you think we forgot you? We would never do that!"

"Speak for yourself, Tory." Their brother Fred appeared, looking even taller than Nate remembered. "Nathan," he said grimly.

"Fred," Nate replied.

Pa's driver, Patrick, approached without a word. Was he still angry? *If he looks at me,* Nate thought, *I'll say hello.* Patrick kept his eyes off Nate and headed straight for the trunk. Nate reached for a leather strap, but Patrick quickly hefted the trunk onto his shoulder and carried it to the carriage.

"I *am* happy to see you, Natey." Tory slipped her arm through his and kissed his cheek. "I've worried so since Pa told us. Are you all right?"

"I'm dandy." He helped her into the carriage, then climbed up.

"Well, idiot," Fred said, hopping in. "You've outdone yourself this time."

"Hush, Fred." Tory patted Nate's hand as the carriage moved forward.

"No use babying him. Nathan, Pa's madder than I've ever seen him. You'll spend your summer picking slate, is my guess."

"I'm not afraid of Pa," Nate said defiantly.

Fred burst out laughing. "Oh, no? Won't he like *that* news!"

"Don't tell, Fred," Tory pleaded. "Don't cause more trouble."

"I meant what I said," Nate snapped. "Let him tell if he wants to."

Fred leaned over, taking Nate's knee in a painful pinch. "One question: should I pound you now, or wait till after dinner?"

Nate swatted at his hand. "I'm not scared of you, either."

As Fred lunged for him, Tory intervened with a yelp. "Stop it! Both of you!"

Turning away, Nate stared out the window.

"Let him be, Fred. He's had a hard day."

"And who's to blame for that?" Fred mumbled, but said no more.

Their stepmother rushed to Nate in the front hall, full of cheer. "Welcome home, dear." She held his shoulders, kissed his cheek.

"'Lo, Anna." Nate ducked his head, feeling himself blush.

"He's exhausted," Tory said.

Anna nodded. "He *looks* it . . . Well, a good dinner and an early bed, then a fresh start tomorrow, yes, Nate?"

"Okay."

"Dinner in a few minutes."

"All right." He started up the broad, winding staircase.

"Martin and James are ready for bed," Anna added. "They'd love to see their big brother."

"Okay," he called. But he went straight to the third floor, passed the billiard room, and shut himself in his bedroom. He dropped onto the carved-mahogany bed with a sigh, stroking the smooth blue spread. It would be good to lie down, just for a moment, and close his eyes.

A sharp knock knotted his stomach: Pa. "Come in," he said, disgusted by the warble in his words.

Fortunately, it wasn't Pa. But unfortunately, it was Patrick, who carried in the trunk with Harry, the groundskeeper.

"Hallo, Nate!" Harry said. "Good to see you."

"'Lo, Harry."

"Where would you like it, then?"

"Oh, right there's fine." Nate pointed; they set the trunk at the foot of the bed.

Harry gave him a wink. "'Night, now."

"'Night, Harry." Nate watched them both go.

Was Patrick planning to stay mad forever? Just because Nate had ridden his bicycle in front of the brougham at Easter? He was only trying to be funny—how was he to know it would spook the horses? That was precisely why he didn't like animals. They were so unpredictable. His bike did exactly what he made it do. And if it broke down, he fixed it. You couldn't say that about a horse.

He supposed Patrick had a right to be angry about ending up in the ditch. But there were no injuries, no real harm. Patrick had yelled like a banshee and told Pa on him. Wasn't that revenge enough? And it had happened two months ago! Why couldn't he just forget the whole thing? Not that Nate cared. But Patrick was a servant in this house—who was he to show Nate his anger, or bear a grudge against him?

Nate pulled open the wardrobe door and nearly crawled inside, inhaling the sharp camphor smell. When his fingers found the cherry-wood box behind hanging coats and folded sweaters, he sighed with relief. The dinner bell sounded. He pushed the box farther back and shut the wardrobe.

Tory was waiting near the case clock in the front hall, her smile bright and anxious. "Hungry, Natey?"

"Fred's right, you don't need to baby me," he grumbled, brushing past. But he let her take the lead into the dining room.

Stopping at the head of the table, Tory kissed Pa. "Hello, Papa."

"Good day at school, sweetheart?"

"Yes, Pa, thank you."

Nate skulked behind her, fixing his eyes on the oil portrait of his great-grandfather. As Tory went to her seat, Nate stepped up to Pa's.

"Nathan," Pa said.

"'Lo, Pa."

"How was your journey?"

"Fine, thank you."

Pa nodded him away; Nate took his place between Fred and Tory.

Millie and Winnie, who were eight, sat opposite. With their matching dresses, hazel eyes, and blond hair, Nate never could tell one from the other. They stared with identical stares.

"Hello," Nate said.

They touched heads, giggling.

"Girls," Anna scolded them gently.

Nate smoothed the linen napkin on his lap. Everyone was looking at him, thinking about him. Suddenly he wasn't the least bit hungry.

His oldest brother, Tom, strode in. "Sorry I'm late, Pa. Hello, Mother."

"Hello, Tom."

Mother. Nate clenched his jaw. He could understand the twins—they were only three when Mama died. But why should the rest of them call her Mother? She'd been hired as governess after Mama's death; a year later, Pa married her. Nate would never call her Mother. His mother was gone.

"I was held up at Lattimer," Tom explained. "The breaker boys threw—"

Pa interrupted him. "Not at the table, Tom."

"Right. Sorry, Pa." He saw Nate when he sat down. "Oh, hello there."

"'Lo, Tom."

"Smile, Nate." Tom shook out his napkin, then pushed up the corners of his mouth with his thumb and index finger. "It's not terribly difficult."

Nate stared at him, then turned away.

Pa said grace. Mary, their cook, served roast pork with potatoes and asparagus and her fresh, warm bread. But Nate's mouth was so dry, he could barely chew.

"Oh, Mother, James was *darling* at bedtime," Tory said. "When he says my name it comes out *Toe-eee,* and he's terribly proud of himself!"

"Yes, he is, isn't he?" Anna said with a smile.

"And Pa, I was holding him in the window seat when you arrived. He was calling 'Pa-pa, Pa-pa.' Pressing his little finger on the glass . . ."

Tory's high, quick voice told Nate she was talking from nervousness. It made him feel even more conspicuous; he wished she would shut up. He stuck his fingers in his collar, pulling it from his neck. He chewed a piece of meat twenty-five times before he was able to swallow. He drank half a glass of water.

"Oh, Fred, did you tell Pa what happened on the way to the station?" Tory babbled. "We were *so* late for Nate's train, we—"

Nate could bear it no longer. "Tory!" he said sharply.

Every head turned. Every eye fixed on him. The chill was far worse than the chatter. "Nathan?" Pa questioned.

Nate sat back, biting his lower lip, rubbing his forehead. "Sorry, Tor," he mumbled.

The meal was completed in excruciating silence.

3

"I'LL TAKE COFFEE in the library, please, Mary," Pa said at last, rising. "Nathan."

Nate trailed behind, feeling sick. He was never comfortable alone with Pa, but tonight he was *really* in for it.

"Shut the door," Pa commanded, settling into his armchair. "Sit."

Nate obeyed, and waited. He counted thirty-six ovals in the Oriental carpet's pattern. He glanced at Pa, who was reading a letter—*the* letter, no doubt, from Headmaster. Folding his arms, Nate examined a row of leather-bound books. When he looked back, Pa was glaring right at him, stroking his trim mustache. *"Dear Mr. Tanner,"* he said deliberately. And then he looked down:

> *"It grieves me to write this letter, which informs you of*
> *my intent to expel Nathan from the Brock School.*
> *Numerous incidents have contributed to my decision.*
> *However, yesterday's events so far surpassed the boundaries*
> *of acceptable behavior that I find myself with no other course*
> *of action."*

Pa paused. "What do you suppose went through my mind when I read this?"

That you wished I was dead? Nate wanted to say. He picked at the thread on a waistcoat button.

"It's a beautiful June morning, I collect my mail, proceed to my office—hallo, what's this? *'It grieves me to write this letter.'* Nathan, what do you believe my thoughts might have been?" Pa was using his forced-calm voice, as if phony sincerity could hide his disdain.

Nate did not look up. "I . . . I don't know."

"You don't know." Pa cleared his throat.

"It seems Mr. Fletcher questioned Nathan about his late arrival to Latin class. Nathan said he had gone to retrieve his forgotten grammar, but was unable to produce a monitor's pass and began to remonstrate. I have ascertained, through interviews with Mr. Fletcher as well as with several boys whose character I judge to be most honest and fair, that Nathan's demeanor was shamefully disrespectful. The most egregious charge leveled—and corroborated—was that he threatened Mr. Fletcher with physical harm. Furthermore, Nathan threw a book stand across the room, left school grounds, and did not return until late in the evening."

Pa looked hard at Nate. "Do you dispute this account, Nathan, in any way?"

Nate disputed the account in many ways. But to say so would only draw out his torment. On the train this afternoon, he had promised himself he would not argue with Pa again. He could never win, anyway. And backtalk only made Pa angrier. This summer, at last, he would shut his mouth.

"No, Pa."

*"At this time I met with Nathan. He showed no remorse,
nor did he attempt to defend his behavior. I ended the
interview with expulsion the only option."*

A knock, and Mary entered with Pa's coffee. When Nate
lifted his eyes, she gave him a sympathetic smile. He looked
away. Pa thanked her. She left.

Pa sipped his coffee, then read:

*"I regret that the Brock School has been unable to meet your
hopes regarding Nathan. I believed we could provide a positive
atmosphere in which he would learn and grow. However, as
you know, there have been problems from the start.*

*"Nathan breaks every rule set before him, almost, it
seems, as a point of pride. In his studies he refuses to apply
himself, which is all the more shameful considering the
sharpness of his mind. He is insolent in his dealings with
teachers and fractious with the other boys. I don't believe
Nathan has made any friends since September, except
among a rough set of town boys. I suspect they care more
for Nathan's allowance than they do for him."*

At this Nate lifted his head sharply and opened his mouth
to protest. Of course Pa didn't notice, and droned on:

*"I am sorry to take this action so near to the end of term,
but in my estimation it would compromise the school's*

integrity to keep Nathan. Please arrange his departure at
your earliest convenience . . ."

Pa laid the letter aside. "Et cetera, et cetera." He drank
more coffee. Nate shifted his weight and frowned at his
shoes. "Well," Pa said. "What now?"

Nate slowly lifted his shoulders, then let them drop.

Pa stood. "Get up, Nathan."

This was it: Pa would whip him now. Nate set his teeth
and pushed himself out of the chair, but Pa didn't fetch the
leather strap. He took Nate's shoulders and turned him to
face the big gilt-framed mirror. "Look at yourself, Nathan.
What do you see?"

Nate cast his eyes down. But Pa lifted his chin so that Nate
had to stare at the dull-blue eyes, the wild, mud-colored
hair, and the pasty skin. He hated his face.

Pa said, "I see a twelve-year-old whose time has come to
turn over a new leaf. You're no longer a child, Nathan. You
cannot continue to bring shame and dishonor to this family and to yourself." Pa tightened his grip. "*My* son compromise a school's integrity? I never thought I'd see that day,
Nathan, and I'll be damned if I see another. Do you understand me?"

"Yes."

Pa released him. "You're to go across the street first thing
tomorrow. *You'll* be the one to tell your grandfather what
you've done. Do you hear?"

Nate nodded.

"I've engaged a tutor. Starting next Monday, he'll work

with you from nine until luncheon, five days a week, on Latin, mathematics, and whatever else he deems necessary."

"All summer?" Nate dared to ask.

"Yes, Nate, all summer, by God!" Pa snapped. "Or you won't be able to move ahead in the fall. Is that so difficult to grasp?"

Head down, Nate fumbled with his waistcoat buttons.

"Go to bed now," Pa said more quietly. "We'll start fresh tomorrow, shall we?"

Nate walked quickly to the door, but just as he grabbed the shiny brass handle, Pa called, "Oh, Nathan? One more thing."

"Yes, Pa?" he asked without turning.

"I don't want you to be afraid of me," Pa said deliberately. "I simply want you to obey me."

Nate didn't answer.

"Good night."

"'Night," Nate said, and made a quick getaway up the back stairs.

He switched on the brass lamps with the blue glass shades, locked his door, and changed into his pajamas, leaving his clothes where they fell. It was only half past eight, but he didn't care. He wanted this day over—only sleep could clear away the bad feelings that had begun piling up the moment he'd awakened.

Unlocking his trunk, he pulled out suits and shoes, shirts and pants, tossing them all on the floor, until he found his mother's picture. At school he'd kept the photograph there at the bottom, taking it out only for a brief look when no one was around. He didn't want to be asked about his mother or ridiculed for keeping her photo. But now he held it in both hands. Mama looked so pretty—her gentle smile, her hair pinned up just as he remembered, wisps falling down. It seemed that he could touch her soft brown hair, that her eyes were staring lovingly into his.

He set the picture on his nightstand and closed the silk draperies on the four big windows of his corner room. Then he took the carved box from the wardrobe and sat in the middle of the bed, pulling the sheet up over his head to make a dimly lit tent.

Nate opened the box and took out the lead soldiers—twenty Yanks, twenty Rebels—and fought the Battle Above the Clouds as Grandpa had told it many times: the night spent clinging to the rocky side of Lookout Mountain as cold November rain pelted him; the indescribable noise and confusion in the heat of the fight; the struggle to the top through blinding gun smoke as the Rebels rolled great boulders down at them.

If Fred knew that Nate still played with toy soldiers, there would be no end of torment. Nate hadn't dared bring them to school, not even hidden in his trunk. His roommates would have taken the soldiers for sure, melted them down or thrown them in the river. The soldiers were safer at home— and someday he would stop playing with them. Someday soon.

He had missed them those long months since September; he'd been allowed to come home only for one week at Christmas and one at Easter. Tired as he was, he played out the battle before turning off the lights. But as he lay with his arm around the box and his eyes closed, he remembered Headmaster's letter.

Everything Nate had said and done had been twisted around. Threatening Fletcher? What nonsense. He'd only meant to imply that Pa might take his side and get Fletcher into trouble for beating him. Which was stupid, anyhow. Because Pa never took his side in anything. And that part about him showing no remorse—*What have you to say for yourself, Nathan? Hmm?* Headmaster had asked him in the office. *How do you answer to these very serious charges? Hmm?*— Nate hadn't responded because he was afraid he might cry. Didn't it just figure Headmaster wouldn't see that.

But there was something in the letter worse than all the rest combined: what Headmaster said about his friends in town. Just because Nate shared his allowance didn't mean it was the *reason* for their friendship. And how did Headmaster even know he gave the boys money? How *could* he know, unless he heard it from Brock students? So his friends must have told the Brock fellows. Now he remembered that when he'd run from school, he'd found his friends on the usual corner. He hadn't expected to go into town, so he had no money in his pockets. Suddenly, each boy remembered that he had to go somewhere. And next time Nate saw them, no one seemed too bothered when he said he'd been expelled.

Nate pulled the covers to his chin. *Fresh start tomorrow.* He could practically hear Pa and Anna rehearsing what they ought to say. But there could be no fresh starts for him, not at school in September, not here now. Angrily he rubbed away tears before they had a chance to escape. He propped himself up on an elbow and punched his pillow until he ran out of energy, and then, at last, he slept.

4

THE BREAKER WHISTLE BLEW at five-thirty: the miners' alarm clock. Nate moaned and buried his head beneath the pillow. Why couldn't they fix the whistles so that they were heard only in the patch towns, where the miners lived, and let the rest of the world sleep? After twelve years, he told himself, he ought to be accustomed to it. He pulled the blankets over his head. Next thing he knew, it was past nine.

"Y've missed breakfast," Mary said when he walked into the kitchen. She was standing by the sink, drying plates. "Y've missed it completely, and y' needn't think I'll cook another."

"Did I ask you?" he said, sliding into a chair.

"I'll make y' some toast and tea, if y' like, though, that I'll do."

"Don't trouble yourself."

She clucked her tongue against her teeth. "Right off with the nasty remarks. I'd give that smart mouth o' y'rs a slap, Nathan, if y' were mine."

Nate let Mary talk to him that way only because Mama

had liked her so much. Mary had been with the family ten years, starting when she was sixteen and new to this country. Mama often had been in the kitchen with her, talking and laughing, helping with the baking. While Mama and Mary kneaded, Nate and Tory sat at their own little table fashioning chunks of dough into tiny people, houses, dogs, trees.

Mary put the kettle on. She took a loaf from the bread box, cut two thick slices, and toasted the bread.

"Patrick didn't so much as look at me," Nate told her. "Is he planning to stay mad forever?"

Mary waved a hand. "Ah, y' know the Irish," she said, as if she wasn't one herself. "Keep a grudge till the day of judgment, they will."

"Well, he ought to remember who works for whom around here."

She marched over to him, hands on her hips. "And just *who* do y' think works for *you,* young man? Eh?" she demanded, head bobbing. "How d' y' think y'r da might like to hear about this conversation?" Nate stayed silent, and she turned away: "Ooh, I swear I'd lay y' flat if y' were mine!"

"That's *two* good reasons to be glad I'm not yours," he muttered, propping his elbow on the table, chin on his fist.

Mary ignored him and continued, "And maybe that's what Pat ought to've done that day, make quick work of it and be finished with the whole shebang. Then p'rhaps he'd be talkin' to y' again."

"Let him just try putting a hand on me."

"Elbow off the table," Mary snapped, helping it with a push.

"Hey!"

She slapped the toast on a plate and clapped the plate on the table. She brought him knife, spoon, napkin, butter, and marmalade. The kettle whistled, and she fixed his tea while he buttered the toast.

"Y' know y'r trouble, Nathan?" she asked, placing the cup before him.

"I suspect you're about to inform me," he replied in a bored voice, spooning up the marmalade.

"No." She dropped wearily into a chair across from him. "I've absolutely no idea! I thought maybe *you'd* tell *me!*"

He looked at her. She smiled with more than her eyes this time, and he smiled back—or thought he did.

Mary shook her head sadly. "Ah, look at y', Nate. Y' don't even know how to smile properly anymore."

Then he scowled and leaned his elbow on the table again. He followed a bite of toast with a drink of tea.

"Sweet enough?" Mary asked.

"Perfect."

"It might help if y' told Patrick y' were sorry."

Apologize? Nate didn't see why he should. Maybe Patrick should apologize to *him* for making such a big deal over nothing. Pa had been so angry, he'd locked up Nate's new bicycle.

"Oh, well," Mary said. She got up and returned to her work.

He was still eating when Anna came in. "Good morning, Nate. Sleep well?"

"Yes. Anna?" He looked at her.

"Yes, dear?"

"Can I have my bicycle back? I—"

"Now, Nathan . . ."

"I have nothing to do, and if I could have my bike I—"

"Nate, I cannot make that decision," she said firmly. "You must ask your father."

Nate gave an exaggerated sigh. "Well, what am I supposed to do all day? Then people wonder why I get into trouble."

"For one thing, you could play with your little brothers for a while."

He didn't bother to respond. Anna was always trying to push her boys on him. He didn't like babies, and besides, they were too little to remember him from one visit home to the next.

"Or," Anna said patiently, "you could unpack your trunk."

"Me? Why can't Fiona do it?"

Mary, at the counter with her back to them, gave an indignant snort.

"Mary . . ." Anna sounded exasperated.

"Sorry," Mary said in a small voice.

"Nate, would you come out to the porch?" Anna asked as she stood up.

Outside, he pushed the last bit of toast into his mouth and slumped into a white wicker chair, anticipating the heart-to-heart talk.

"Oh, Nate." Anna sat close and leaned forward. "Can't we be friends? I'll try harder if you will."

He looked at the gray-painted floor, drumming his fingers on his knee.

"I can't bear such an unhappy atmosphere, everyone walking on eggshells."

"Whenever I'm around, right?"

"It needn't be that way," she answered, touching his sleeve.

He pulled away. "Don't worry, Anna. You'll only have to put up with it till September. He'll find another school to ship me off to."

"That needn't be, either," she said softly. "It's *your* behavior, Nate. You can change it."

He launched himself from the chair and started down the wide steps.

"Nate," Anna called, "your father asked me to remind you to see your grandfather."

Nate kept walking. If he went to Grandpa's, he'd probably just have to listen to more criticism. It would make him feel even worse.

You must ask your father. Pa would hold that bicycle over his head the rest of his life, in all likelihood. How long would he have to suffer for one small mistake?

But no matter. He would show them he didn't need a bicycle. His own two feet could take him just as far, if not as fast. Nate walked across the lush lawn, through the iron gate, and onto the sidewalk.

He would go where he wanted, and return when he pleased.

5

"NATHAN!" Tory brightened when she saw him later that afternoon. She took his hand. "What a nice surprise! I'm waiting for the twins. Will you walk us home?"

"I'll go partway, I guess."

She frowned, searching his face. "What's wrong?"

Millie and Winnie ran through the school doors. "Do you know who I am?" one of them asked Nate.

"I have no idea," he admitted.

Both twins giggled furiously.

"It's simple," Tory said, pointing. "That's Millie. She has extra freckles on her nose and a rounder face."

"I do not!" Millie protested.

"And she's cuter," Tory added, pinching her cheek.

"She is not!" Winnie said.

"I'm just teasing, silly!" The twins raced ahead, and Tory slipped her arm through Nate's. "What did you do today?"

"I argued with Anna and I didn't see Grandpa," he told her. "And I didn't go home for lunch."

"You had no lunch?"

"I bought candy. And a soda water."

They walked in silence.

"I hate to see you getting off on the wrong foot," Tory said gently. "Why did you and Mother quarrel?"

"Oh, never mind," he mumbled. "Listen, I only came to tell you I'm sorry. For snapping last night."

"That's all right. I know you were upset." She squeezed his arm. "Come home, Nate, I'll—"

"No!" he interrupted, and she said no more.

In the park, boys were gathering—enough for two baseball teams, it looked like. Nate's cousin George was there, with others he'd known for years.

Tory gave him a nudge. "Why don't you play?"

"Nah." He shrugged. "I don't feel like it."

"Oh, go on, Nate," she urged.

He didn't want to seem pathetic, and he *did* want to play. Maybe this summer would be different. He released Tory's arm, breaking into a run. "See you later, Tor!"

"Don't be late for dinner!" she called.

When the boys saw him, they looked surprised—and not too happy.

"Nate!" His cousin managed a weak smile. "Your school's out already?"

"Yeah. Hi, George. Who's captains?"

"Will and Louis."

Nate pretended not to notice the silence. "Can I play?"

"Well, uh, we already chose sides," Will said, going red in the face.

"Yeah, Nate, and, um, you don't have your glove," Louis added.

Nate turned toward the road. Was Tory observing this reception? No, she had gone. "I can use somebody else's," he said.

Will and Louis looked at George for help. "Nate, you always make trouble," George said.

"I won't," Nate promised.

"You always say that, too," Will reminded him.

"Yeah," Louis said, and the others muttered in agreement. George met Nate's gaze and shrugged, turning up his palms.

"I'm a better player than all of you!" Nate said.

"Who cares?" George replied. "We just want to have fun."

"Yeah, and we never do when you're around," Will added. This time everyone laughed.

Nate yanked Will's glove from his hand and threw it to the ground. Will grabbed him by the shirt. Nate bunched his hands into fists, but George got between them.

"Let him go, Will," George said, and Will did. George shook his head at Nate. "Just get away, Nate, will you? Leave us alone." He retrieved Will's glove and turned his back to Nate, walking toward the field. Louis, Will, and the others followed.

Nate wanted to light into them and start hitting, hitting anyone, everyone. Instead he picked up a stone and threw it at George's shoes. Without waiting for the reaction, he ran away.

6

NATE WAS NOT ALLOWED near any of the family's ten breakers—towering, blackened wooden buildings where coal was broken up and sorted after it was blasted from the mines below. The collieries were dirty and dangerous, no place for children, Pa said. But Nate figured he'd done just about everything else wrong since he'd opened his eyes this morning. Might as well make a day of it. *We'll start fresh tomorrow, shall we?*

Near the Harland breaker, he watched, warily, from a distance; someone in the family might be around. As the coal cars came up from the mine tunnels, they were towed to the top of the breaker. Inside, the coal was tipped down chutes, and workers called breaker boys picked out the slate and wood that got mixed in during blasting. Then the coal tumbled down to the bottom, where men shoveled it into train cars whose tracks ran from the colliery through the patch town, and on to the cities.

Slowly Nate edged closer, awaiting the whistle that ended the workday. Alongside the breaker were culm banks, massive hills of slate picked out by the breaker boys. Usable coal was often discarded by accident, and now girls were wandering about, climbing the hills, sifting through the filthy culm for coal to burn in kitchen stoves.

They were the miners' daughters, and they weren't supposed to be there. Nate had overheard Pa grumbling about how it was impossible to keep the wives and daughters off the culm banks. Warning signs were posted; guards often patrolled. Still, the families paid no attention. But should a bank slide and bury someone alive, Pa said, they expected the company to shoulder the blame.

The girls gathered coal in scuttles, then deposited it in a wagon or wheelbarrow. Little brothers and sisters played on the banks, too, free and wild. Nate thought of Anna's boys, shadowed every moment.

At last a man came from the colliery office, shouting and waving. With no sign of alarm, the girls gathered the children and headed home.

Nate carefully skirted the culm banks, then sat hunched behind the last one. He waited so long that his mind wandered, and his heart skipped when he heard the breaker whistle's scream. Getting up, he watched the breaker boys burst through a door about halfway up the side of the breaker. Cheering and shouting, they raced down the rickety wooden stairs, swatting one another with tin lunch pails, pulling stocking caps from their heads and scarves from their faces, which were blackened by coal dust.

The breaker boys were sons of miners. Their fathers and older brothers worked deep below the surface. Nate knew breaker boys had to be at least twelve years old. As they drew nearer, he saw that they didn't all look twelve. But they did look as if they were having fun. One boy yanked down a smaller one's pants, and they all howled, even the victim.

Some ate leftover lunch as they walked; some pushed and chased one another.

Now the boys were just a few yards away, talking fast, some in a foreign language. They were Slavic immigrants whose parents had come to coal country to make a better life, just as the Irish and Welsh had done before them.

Nate was so intent on watching, he forgot the boys could see him. Then one called, "Hey, kid!" Their eyes met. "Who are *you?*" the boy challenged him, veering in Nate's direction.

Nate ran for the woods, and the breaker boys responded with raucous laughter.

7

ALONG THE ROAD near the Banbury patch town, Nate heard horses. He scuttled into the bushes, but the landau rolled to a halt, and then came Pa's vexed, impatient cry: "Na-*than!*"

Nate stepped into view. Fred and Tom made no attempt to hide their mirth.

"You're not invisible, Nate," Pa said, beckoning to him. "You may *wish* to be, and for good reason, but I regret to inform you that you are quite, quite *there.*"

Nate climbed in next to Pa. Patrick clucked, and the carriage jerked ahead.

Pa started right in. "Nathan, I believe I've tolerated a great deal from you. But I *will* not brook flagrant disobedience. Were you not specifically told to see your grandfather this morning?"

"Yes, Pa," he said, looking out at the Banbury breaker.

"Yet when your grandfather arrived at his office, what do you think was the first thing he said to me?"

Pa did love his games, but Nate wasn't in the mood to play. He shrugged.

"He said, 'I saw Nathan from my window this morning; you didn't tell me he was home for the summer.' Now, what do you think my reaction might have been?"

"You said I was a mirage?"

Tom and Fred laughed, but Pa clapped his hand hard on Nate's knee, barking, "*Don't* you two encourage him!"

Abruptly, they stopped.

"I don't wish to thrash you, Nathan. But I will if you—" Roughly, Pa gripped Nate's chin between his thumb and forefinger, jerking Nate's head up. "Look at me when I speak to you!"

Nate hated this above all else. Nothing was more humiliating than being forced to look at someone. He stared hard into Pa's fiery eyes.

"I'll have no more defiance and impudence, Nathan," Pa warned him. "Here are the rules you will follow, each and every day. One: You will eat breakfast with the rest of the family, and not be fed toast at whatever hour you make your way to the kitchen. Two: You will not strew your clothing about your room, and you will unpack your *own* trunk. The household staff is not employed for your personal convenience. Three: If you expect to be away from the house at lunchtime, you will inform Mother in a timely fashion. And four:"—Pa stomped his foot on the floorboards—"When I tell you to do something, you will do it! Is there *any*thing I have said that is in *any* way difficult to understand?"

Nate shook his head.

"Pardon me! I did not hear your response!"

"No, Pa."

"Patrick!" Pa called out. "Drive Nathan to his grandfather's door, please. Evidently he needs to be watched like a child."

"Yes, sir."

It was the crowning indignity, to be dressed down in front of a servant—especially Patrick, who was probably snickering smugly as he turned into Grandpa's half-circle drive.

Nate raised his head to look at his brothers. Fred's mouth twisted into a disgusted smirk, but Tom gave him a slight wink. Nate jumped down before the carriage had stopped, and climbed the steps of the stone mansion. He lifted the heavy brass knocker and let it drop, then took off his cap.

The door slowly swung open. "Why, hello, Nathan," said Grandpa's housekeeper, Esther.

"'Lo, Esther."

"Here to see your grandfather?"

Nate nodded, stepping inside.

"I'll tell Colonel Tanner you're here."

While waiting, Nate thought bitterly of Anna's words: *Oh, Nate. Can't we be friends?* Pretending to be so sweet, then stabbing him in the back, telling Pa about the toast and the trunk.

"Your grandfather will see you in the drawing room, Nate," Esther said. "Would you like a nice cold glass of lemonade?"

"Yes, thanks." His throat was parched, and maybe the drink would also take the edge off his fierce hunger. "Grandpa?" Nate said at the drawing-room door.

Grandpa looked up from the *Hazleton Sentinel* and set down his whiskey and soda. "Come here, young fellow, come over here and shake the old man's hand!"

Nate obeyed; Grandpa worked his hand like a pump. "'Lo, Grandpa."

"Sit down, Nathan, right here before me. We have a few things to discuss!"

Nate sat.

"Your father's at sixes and sevens, Nate. Do you know what that means?"

"Yes, Grandpa."

"It means he's all in a dither, he's at a loss, he's completely flummoxed—in short, young man, he doesn't know what to do!"

Esther brought the lemonade in a crystal glass, on a silver tray. She set it down and left.

Nate took a long drink.

"What happened at that school of yours, Nathan? Tell the old colonel. If there's one thing I know about, it's boys. Why, when we were at Chancellorsville, some of my boys cut loose a railroad car with me in it! Off went the train, and there sat the colonel and his staff! They meant nothing by it—high spirits and nerves is all it was. But I had to pretend I was angry, because I was the commander. Never did get to the bottom of that one." Grandpa chuckled and shook his head, staring across the room. Then he seemed to remember Nate. "So, tell me, boy. Get carried away with some friends, did you? Mischief gone awry?"

"No, it was a misunderstanding. I needed a book from—"

"Misunderstanding! Certainly it was! Boys will be boys, though. The headmaster ought to realize that. Still, Nate, it won't do, being expelled from school. You're a Tanner! You'll be a leader of this community one day, same as your father and your uncles and your grandpa and my father before me."

Nate nodded, trying to look solemn.

"I have a multitude of concerns, and a multitude of grandsons to step in and take over. What appeals to you, Nate? Coal? Lumber? Iron?"

"I'm—I'm not sure, Grandpa," Nate mumbled, and sipped more lemonade.

"Coal is our backbone, of course. So you'll start in coal, like all the others. Your brother Fred is to spend the summer learning under me as my clerk. But no grandson of mine will be a clerk for long. Fred will be off to prep school in the fall, and later on he'll earn his engineering degree at your father's alma mater. And Tom is learning to supervise the operations while he's home from college. I want you there, too, in a few years—you and George are next. But we can't do anything with boys who are sent home in shame, Nathan." Grandpa leaned forward. "Do you understand me, son? Look at me, now."

Reluctantly, Nate lifted his eyes. Grandpa wore a deep frown.

"I know you've had . . . upsets. Certain aspects of your childhood. But your mother's five years gone. It's time to put it behind you, Nate."

Nate gulped down his anger with swallows of lemonade. *Put it behind you.* How dare Grandpa talk about Mama that way? As if it could be so easy. As if it should be.

"Stop fighting your father," Grandpa went on. "Show him he can be proud of you. And Anna, of course she'll never take your mother's place in your heart. But she's trying to do right by you. Don't you agree?"

"She told—"

Grandpa interrupted him. "Let's have a pleasant summer within our own family, at least, shall we?" He patted Nate's shoulder. "The good Lord knows there's trouble enough brewing at the collieries."

Nate shot him a look. "Trouble?"

"Ah!" Grandpa sat back and picked up his drink. "It will all straighten itself out. Always does. None of your concern, young fellow. Well, off you go, Nate. Leave the old man to his whiskey and his dinner, and you go ahead to yours— dinner, that is!" he finished, chuckling at his joke.

"Yes, Grandpa." Nate stood.

"Be a good boy, Nathan," Grandpa said. He was back to reading his paper before Nate left the room.

8

A TWO-MASTED SHIP SWUNG BACK AND FORTH, sailing over a metal sea. *Tock. Tock. Tock.* Staring, Nate thought of a hypnotist: *You are sleepy, verrrryy sleeeeppy.* Did they say that in real life, or only in books and theater? The case clock was from way back in Mama's family, from somewhere in Connecticut.

He wandered the rest of the ground floor: the parlor, with its formal, uncomfortable furniture, tasseled draperies, and Oriental carpets; Pa's study, where the big cherry-wood desk was piled with papers; the bright, many-angled conservatory, with windows instead of walls, and plants everywhere; the library, where he would have his lessons. They would start today, as soon as his tutor arrived.

In the paneled drawing room, he sank into a comfortable armchair by the delft-tiled fireplace. At night the leaded-glass lamps created a cozy glow, and Nate liked to sit near the fire in winter, eating popcorn and drinking cocoa, playing checkers or Parcheesi with Tory, cranking the Edison phonograph. Not last winter, though, when he was at school. *Why is it so difficult for you to get along with others?* Headmaster had demanded of him. *Hmm? Must you hit every boy with whom you quarrel? Can you not simply walk away?* That was easier said than done, when boys looked for ways to pick fights, to get him into trouble. It was best to avoid the common room entirely and go straight to his room after dinner. But at lights-out, his roommates taunted him: *What's the matter, Tanner, too good for us?*

Nate pushed himself out of the drawing-room chair with a sigh.

Next to the kitchen was the playroom. When he was little, it was his favorite place, full of toys and paints, a rocking horse and trains. Now it belonged to Martin and James, who were in there with Lucy, the governess. Their voices drove him from the door.

Circling to the dining room, he ran his fingers along the sideboard's smooth marble top. He stopped before the painting of his grandfather's father, a farmer's son who came to the Hazleton area when he was very young to work as a land surveyor.

Nate stared at the man for whom he was named—the man who had, it was said, discovered anthracite in the Lehigh Valley by watching a deer paw at a shiny patch of ground way back in '33. Quietly, as he saved money from his earnings, Great-grandfather Nathan bought coal land all over the region. From nothing but hard work and a hard head, Nathan Tanner made himself a rich man.

The portrait showed a grim-faced man, distinguished and determined-looking. Nate wondered if he himself would ever accomplish anything. Maybe Fletcher had been right about him: When you had so much, what was left to try for?

The doorbell's loud *brrriiiing* made Nate jump. He leaned

on the sideboard, hands behind his back. When the bell sounded again, he went to the kitchen.

"Fee!" Mary called up the back stairs. Her hands were sticky with dough.

"Coming!" Fiona answered.

Mary frowned when she saw him. "D' y' have trouble with y'r ears, Nathan? D' y' not hear the bell?"

"It isn't my job."

"Ooooh!" She shook her head. "What gets *into* y', I'd like to know!"

He sat at the table. Mary said nothing more, just continued mixing the dough.

Fiona came in, saying, "Mary, have you seen— Oh, there you are, Nathan. Your tutor's in the library with Mrs. Tanner."

Nate rose to his feet and shuffled to the library.

"Here he is now." Anna smiled nervously. "Mr. Hawthorne, I'd like to present Nathan."

" 'Lo," Nate said, and bit his lip.

"Nathan," Anna said in her governess voice.

"How do you do, Mr. Hawthorne."

"I'm pleased to meet you, Nathan."

"Well!" Anna clapped her hands once. "I'll leave you to it. Mr. Hawthorne, if you need anything at all, please don't hesitate to ask. Mary will bring refreshments shortly."

"Thank you, Mrs. Tanner."

As soon as she left, Nate flung himself into an armchair and slumped way down.

"Well, Nathan, you have a bit of catching up to do," Mr. Hawthorne said pleasantly, sitting at the writing desk.

"So I hear," Nate mumbled to the floor.

"And whether you do it is entirely up to you, as far as I'm concerned."

Nate looked up.

"I don't intend to spend five mornings a week badgering you, because it does not matter to me whether you're held back or you move ahead." He was entirely cheerful about it, and it wasn't even the sarcastic cheer Nate was accustomed to from schoolmasters. "I'll assign your work, and you will know exactly what I expect of you. If you don't meet those expectations, it's between you and your father."

"Well, what is it you expect?" Nate asked, sitting up.

"I have a full report here from your former headmaster—"

Nate made a face. "You do?"

"Yes. And from that I've devised a lesson plan in Latin, arithmetic, literature, and recitation."

"Recitation?" Nate repeated with distaste.

"I'll help you memorize one long poem, and I'll ask you to recite it in full on our last day together."

"Ugghhh." Nate sighed, slouching again. "I hate poetry."

"No, you don't." Mr. Hawthorne sounded pretty confident, considering that they'd met just five minutes ago. "You only hate certain poems."

"Like that Coleridge somebody. I'm not reciting anything like 'The Wedding-Guest he beat his breast,'" Nate warned him.

Mr. Hawthorne laughed heartily. "You'll be choosing

your own poem. And I'll bet you find one you like right here," he said, tapping a book.

"Oh, yeah? What'll you bet?"

"Well, I'm not sure." Mr. Hawthorne's puzzled tone made Nate grin. "I think we can make this a pleasant experience, Nathan. We don't need to stay stuck indoors. I imagine you'll conjugate Latin just as well outside as you would in this room, for instance."

"I imagine you're right."

"All right, then. Shall we begin?"

Nate nodded toward the desk. "Let me see that book."

Mr. Hawthorne raised his brows.

"Please," Nate added.

His tutor smiled.

9

NATE FIGURED HE WAS the only boy since 1777 who hated the Fourth of July. That was when Grandpa gave his annual lawn party for family and friends, which also meant George's friends, and Tory's friends, and Fred's friends, and the friends of everybody else but Nate. It was the day above all others that shouted his insignificance.

If only he could blame everything on Mama's death. But he had never gotten along with other boys, really. Mama was the only one who had understood. She didn't ridicule or shout at him about it, and when he got into a scrape, she always listened to his side.

Something else had made the party tolerable when Mama was alive: knowing that the following day they'd leave Hazleton to spend the summer at their country house—for the most part without Pa, who came only on weekends and for two weeks in August. Nate loved picnicking in the woods and playing Robin Hood with Tory, swinging into the creek on a thick rope. Mama had adored the country, too, but soon after she died, Pa sold the house. It grieved him to go there without Mama, he'd said. But his grief seemed to disappear as soon as Anna entered their lives.

Anna preferred the shore. But they went for only two weeks each August because Anna claimed she couldn't bear to be away from Pa, and Pa claimed he couldn't be away from the coal.

Now the Fourth was a day-long jab in the ribs, reminding Nate of all he had lost.

"Well, Nathan," Pa said as the family crossed the street to Grandpa's, "let's see if you can make it through the day without injuring anyone, hmm?"

"You can stay with me, Natey," Tory whispered, but he just scowled in reply.

Grandpa's grounds were even larger, his gardens more elaborate than the ones at home. Long tables were draped in white linen cloths; stars-and-stripes bunting hung from the back of the house. Servants streamed from the kitchen, bearing large platters and bowls. There was cold roast beef and fried chicken, salads, aspics, and sweet gelatins. Nate ate too much and too slowly, deliberately wasting time.

Later he walked the perimeter of the festivities, trying to look as if he had things to do, people who cared. Other years, Tom had taken pity on him and played tennis with him for a quarter of an hour. Nate pretended to like it, just for something to do. But the only person Tom noticed these days was Alice Parker.

The first Fourth of July after Mama died, Tory clasped Nate's hand and took him around with her. She was only a year older, and they had always been close. Yet now they were growing apart. Tory was still kind to him—too kind, even. But at thirteen, she had no interest in cowboys and Indians, hide-and-seek, climbing trees. Today she huddled with her girl friends and cousins, whispering and twittering. It seemed everywhere Nate went lately—Jacobs' for a lemon ice, People's Drug for candy, Hazle Park—there were huddles of giggling girls. What could be so funny all the time?

At Grandpa's party, vanilla ice cream was always hand-cranked in a big freezer. It was the children's job to turn the handle continually, until the ice cream was ready. Another way Nate passed the time was by taking as many turns as he could.

"Oh, Nathan! You're our *best* ice-cream cranker!" Aunt Bess gushed, bustling to his side. George's mother often took it upon herself to tend to Nate, treating him like a pathetic motherless child. He cringed inwardly whenever she came near. "But you're working too hard, dear!"

"That's all right," he mumbled. "I like it."

"Nonsense! Go play with the boys, Nate. They're about to start the games."

Nate hated "the games" most of all. Sack races, egg-on-spoon races, relays—they infuriated him because the others never took them seriously, flagrantly cheating in the name of "fun," or dissolving into fits of laughter in the midst of a contest. Last year it ended in a fight, and a scolding from Pa, and Nate skulking off to read *Treasure Island* in Grandpa's library until the fireworks began.

"No, thanks," he said with a plastered smile. "I'd rather do this."

"Don't be silly, Nate!" Aunt Bess looked around until her eyes lit upon her son. "Georgie! Georgie, take Nate with you to the games."

George eyed him distastefully.

"No, Aunt Bess, really . . ."

Aunt Bess nudged him away, taking hold of the crank. "I haven't done this in years!" she crowed. "What *fun*! Run along, boys!"

"Come on," George said in a voice soaked with resentment.

Nate trailed behind him and Will and Louis.

"So, Nate"—Will turned to walk backwards—"we heard you got kicked out of school."

Nate shot a look at George, who ricocheted it to Will.

"What of it?" Nate snapped.

"Never mind, never mind," Will said quickly.

Nate persisted. "No, go on, what else? You know *why* I got expelled?"

No one spoke.

"'Cause I beat a fellow so bad he went to the hospital. George tell you that, too?"

Just as Nate thought, and hoped, George couldn't stop himself: "That's a lie, Nate. Your father told mine you got kicked out because you threatened a teacher."

"That's right. And I'd've done it, too. Killed him." Even as he spoke, he felt ridiculous. But he kept on: "I had it all planned out, just how I'd do it."

The others exchanged glances. George waved a dismissive hand: "Shut up, Nate."

"Yeah, big talker," Will said.

"How *would* you have done it, Nate? Thrown a rock at his shoes, then run off?" Louis added, and all three guffawed.

The white-hot light burned Nate's eyes, and the next thing he knew, he and Louis were rolling on the ground.

"Get off me!" Louis hissed, pushing him away. Louis scrambled to his feet, brushing himself off.

Nate did the same, looking around. Nobody, fortunately, had noticed.

"You behave like the Hunkies and Dagos in the patches," George said contemptuously. "Attacking like an animal. Can't you ever control yourself?"

In response, Nate stormed across the lawn and off Grandpa's grounds. Everybody knew that the Slavs and Italians who worked in the mines were coarse and vulgar people who spent all their spare time getting drunk, gambling, and fighting. George had some nerve, comparing Nate to those dirty foreigners.

For a while he stomped around the house, angrily slamming doors and kicking walls. When he felt calmer, he retrieved his ball and glove and threw himself pop flies in the back yard, pretending he was playing for the Philadelphia Phillies.

After a while, there was an odd comfort to being home by himself. Any time now, someone would come for him—Tory, or maybe Anna. Perhaps Grandpa would ask, *Now, where did Nathan get off to?* He watched the goldfish in the little pond, climbed the massive copper beech in the far corner near the fence, and wended his way through the maze of yew trees.

But eventually the familiar chill of loneliness settled in. No one missed him. He was utterly invisible.

Around now, Grandpa would be making a stirring speech about independence and freedom and the preservation of the glorious Union. Up in his room, Nate allowed the Rebels a clear victory at Antietam, letting them sweep through the cornfield with a fierce vengeance, laying waste to everything along Bloody Lane.

It was dusk. The last of the ice cream was probably being scooped, served with juicy strawberries. Nate thought with longing of the dessert table: triple-layer chocolate tortes, apple pies, white cakes with feathery coconut icing, tangy cherry tarts, chewy macaroons, crunchy meringues. He told himself to go back. If no one knew he had been gone, they wouldn't notice his return. But he couldn't force his feet across the floor.

Instead, he lay on the front-hall carpet, staring up at the carved-oak ceiling. Perhaps Pa would come, saying, *What in the world are you doing, Nate?* His tone would be kind but puzzled, and then he'd ask Nate nicely to come back to the party with him . . .

Nate shook his head. "Sure," he muttered.

Soon after Mama's clock had bonged nine times, the fireworks began. Now everyone would be watching from Grandpa's front lawn and porch, the boys setting off the smaller fireworks Grandpa had ordered: Roman candles and skyrockets and salutes. If Nate walked out to his front porch, they would all be able to see him. But up on the roof, at the back of the house, he would have a perfect view. He went to the trunk room on the third floor and climbed out the window.

Fireworks shocked the sky over the Hazle Park lake with pink streaks, blue fireballs, white sunbursts, red lightning. Blurred by his tears, they were more beautiful than ever.

10

"NA-*THAN*!"

Nate went to the window. Pa stood on the front lawn, looking around, hands on hips. Nate's stomach tightened. Now what? He had been eating breakfast with the family, cleaning his room, studying with Mr. Hawthorne, staying away from the breakers. And when he walked by the base-ball field, he didn't even look at George and the others.

He had been good. Good and bored. So what was Pa calling him for?

Pa turned to the porch. "Where *is* that boy?"

Nate unhooked the screen and stuck his head out. "Yes, Pa?"

Pa looked up. "What in heaven's name are you doing shut up inside on a beautiful Saturday morning? Come down here, Nate!"

"Yes, Pa." Nate scooped his soldiers into their box and put them away.

Anna was on the porch, looking at a magazine. Martin and James were playing with blocks. And then something amazing happened: Pa turned to Nate and smiled.

"Well, Nate . . ." Pa swept out his arm. There, propped against the porch rail, was Nate's bicycle. He stole a quick look at Pa, who said, "You may have it back."

"Honest?" Nate dared not step toward it. No doubt Pa was about to say he must do something odious first. Apologize to Patrick, or play with Anna's boys.

"Honest" was all Pa said.

"You mean ride it and everything?"

"Ride it and everything." Pa chuckled. "Harry's even pumped up the tires."

"Thank you, Pa. *Thank* you."

Pa gestured toward Anna. "Thank Mother. It was her idea."

"Oh, Thomas," Anna said.

"She believes you'll live up to responsibility if it's given to you, Nate, and I had to be persuaded of that." Pa was looking stern now.

"I will, Pa," Nate said seriously. "I promise. And thank you, Anna."

"You're quite welcome," Anna said. "Well, go ahead, dear."

"Yes, have a nice long ride," Pa agreed. "On a day like this, I suppose a boy could ride for miles."

"I suppose you're right!" Nate dashed inside and grabbed his brown cap from the rack. Pa offered him a silver dollar; Nate slid it into his pocket. "Thanks, Pa!"

"Home for dinner, yes?" Pa called.

"Yes!" he shouted, already on his way.

He pedaled through the front gate, and when he had ridden beyond the iron picket fence surrounding their grounds, he was giddy with freedom. George and Will and Louis were on the sidewalk, towels draped around their necks, waiting for the trolley to Hazle Park. Who cared? He had his bike back, and he didn't need anybody—least of all that gruesome crew. He coasted down the hill and away from Hazleton at full speed, feet on the handlebars, and when the road flattened, he rode no-handed and one-handed, in wide loops, taking off his cap to let the breeze ruffle his hair. It didn't matter now about school or Pa or Anna or Patrick. He just rode, past High Ridge, past Banbury, past the Harland breaker and the road to Harland patch town.

He decided to look for some huckleberry bushes he'd found last summer, and left his bike in a birch thicket by the road. But when he pushed through the brush and reached the bushes, another boy was already there, wolfing down berries. Nate stopped short, glaring.

The boy was definitely some kind of foreigner. He looked startled, but relaxed right away. "Ah, it's only you," he said with a grin, as if he'd known Nate all his life. "Whatta *you* doin' here?"

"Uh, same as you, I guess." To prove it, Nate plucked a berry.

"Good, ain't they?" the boy said, shoving two into his mouth. His shirt was made of a rough blue fabric, frayed at the neck, mended elsewhere. He wore long pants, not knee pants like Nate, and he was barefoot. "Thought I'd pick some for my mother." He held up a pailful. "I sneaked away. Didn't want nobody else findin' this place." He faced Nate, eyeing him critically. "Why'd you run away from us?" he asked, and only then did Nate realize he was the breaker boy who had spoken to him at the culm bank weeks ago.

"Oh," he said, attempting a casual shrug, "I don't know."

"I oughta run you off again."

So now they would have to fight—of course. Might as well get it over with and ride on. Nate narrowed his eyes, set his jaw, and said in a low growl: "Go ahead and try."

But the boy waved him off. "Aw, I'm just kiddin'." He popped another berry into his mouth. "What's your name, anyway? I'm Johnny."

"Nate."

"Where do you live?"

"Um . . . Hazleton," Nate said reluctantly.

"I live in Harland patch." He cocked his head curiously. "You walked here all the way from Hazleton?"

"No, I rode my bike."

Johnny's eyes lit up. "You got a *bike*? Can I see?"

"Okay." Nate began to lead the way, but Johnny beat him to it.

"Wow!" Johnny ran his hand along the shiny red paint. "That's the best bike I ever saw! Can I try it out?"

"Uh, sure," Nate said, though he didn't feel sure at all. What if Johnny crashed it? Did he know how to ride? He'd be insulted if Nate asked, wouldn't he?

Johnny leaped onto the bike, hooking his bucket over the handlebar, and made it very clear that he *did* know how to ride. Off he went toward the Harland breaker, as Nate watched and waited.

And waited and waited.

But Johnny didn't turn around. And Nate, feeling sick, stared helplessly as Johnny faded from sight.

Already he was rehearsing his words to Pa: *I let a breaker boy ride it and he didn't bring it back.* Fred's laughter, Tory's sympathetic eyes, the giggling of the twins. But much worse, his bicycle was gone. The summer had just been starting to show promise, and now . . . How could he have been so stupid?

At least he knew where Johnny lived and worked. But what of it? What could he do, march into the patch searching for Johnny? Wait outside the breaker? All those boys, ready to fight, Nate was sure, for one another. Wouldn't Pa love to hear he'd fought with a miner's boy!

He started down the road, kicking at stones. When he

looked up, he blinked to be sure of what he was seeing: a glimmer of red—Johnny was riding toward him. He waved; Nate did the same. When Johnny stopped, he said to Nate accusingly, "You thought I wasn't comin' back."

"I did not."

"Sure you did. You started walkin'."

"Well, you went pretty far."

"'Cause it was *fun*," Johnny said, grinning. "Hey, Nate. You play baseball?"

"Yeah."

"Want to play with me and my pals?"

Nate hesitated. There was no sport he liked better than baseball. There was no sport he liked *except* baseball. But he couldn't play with a bunch of breaker boys. It just wouldn't be right. "I—I—I don't have my glove," he stammered.

Johnny's eyebrows shot up. "You have a ball glove, too?"

"Um, yeah."

"You rich?" Johnny asked eagerly.

"Um—uh—no, my grandparents, they live in Philadelphia," he lied. "Well, they're not rich, either, but I'm named for my grandfather. So he buys me stuff sometimes."

"Oh." Johnny sounded disappointed. "Well, where's your father work, then?" He started riding slowly, and Nate walked alongside.

"He, um—" What was a job that didn't pay a lot of money—besides mining? Doctor, lawyer, banker. Money, money, money. He recalled Grandpa saying, *No grandson of mine will be a clerk for long.* "He's a clerk."

"What kind of clerk?"

Nate shrugged. "A regular clerk, I guess."

"Where?" Johnny persisted.

"In—um—at the Edison. The electric company."

"Oh." Johnny got off the bike and leaned it toward Nate. "So, you want to play or not?"

She believes you'll live up to responsibility if it's given to you, Pa had said, and Nate had promised, no more than an hour ago. Promised! Besides, every time he joined in a baseball game, close plays led to punches, and the next thing he knew he was off the field, by force or by choice. Why should it be any different with Johnny and his friends? On the other hand, Johnny hadn't wanted to fight him. So maybe . . . "All right," he said.

"Awright," Johnny echoed, nodding. "Come on, let's go to my house and get gloves."

Go to his house? In the patch? "You—you sounded like you didn't have a glove," Nate said nervously.

"No, we use old work gloves, from our papas," Johnny explained.

Well, Pa had never told Nate not to go near the patch, just the breaker. And Nate *was* curious to see what it was like.

"Come on," he said to Johnny. "Get up on the handlebars."

11

HARLAND WAS HOME to the Slavic miners—mainly people from Slovakia and Poland. At the top of the patch road, the houses were painted and well kept, surrounded by grass and flowers. That was where the managers and superintendents lived, most of them Irishmen who used to be miners. The road was straight and long, and as Nate and Johnny continued riding, the houses grew shabbier, with no shingles or paint, and with tar-paper roofs. There were high wooden fences everywhere.

The bike bumped over the railroad tracks near the company store. Children and dogs poured from houses and alleys, chasing them. Chickens and roosters squawked as they ran out of the way. Nate was sorely embarrassed, but Johnny perched proudly, holding up his hands, nodding right and left as if he were king.

"Right up here," he called to Nate, pointing. "This one here." Nate stopped. "Hey, Joey!" A boy stepped forward. "Here's my little brother," Johnny told Nate, twisting the boy's ear.

What country was Johnny from, anyway? He talked with only the trace of an accent, and he knew all the right English words.

"Hi," Joey said.

"Hi," Nate replied.

"That's Nate's bike. Watch it good, will you? And don't ride it."

"Awright." Joey snatched a huckleberry as Johnny unhooked the pail.

Johnny slapped his head lightly. "Go pick your own. Where's Mama?"

Joey shrugged.

Nate followed Johnny onto a small rickety porch and then inside. The front room was about the same size as the bathroom Nate shared with his brothers. There was a bed, low to the floor, with a plain wooden frame, covered with a colorful quilt. Hanging on the wall above it was a crucifix, like the one Mary had over her bed. In the corner sat a cradle. There was a little chest of drawers. Nothing more.

Next came the kitchen, with board floors and a coal stove and a wooden table with six chairs bunched around it, none matching. Pots and pans hung on hooks. On the wall were framed pictures of Jesus. Wooden shelves held bowls and plates and cups and baskets. Nate had expected that the house would be dirty, but it was neat and clean. A pitcher filled with flowers had been placed on the table, and curtains with bright designs hung from both windows.

Johnny set the berries down. "Come on." They climbed narrow, creaky steps. "That's where my sisters sleep," he said, pointing into a tiny room. "Me and my brothers and—" When he opened the door, he stopped talking.

An older boy sat on a bed, back to the wall, a book propped against his drawn-up knees. "What are you doing, Johnny?" he asked in an accent much thicker than Johnny's.

"This is Nate," Johnny said. "That's my brother Stefan."

"Hi," Nate said.

Stefan nodded pleasantly. "Hello."

"He goes to night school. He don't do nothin' but work and read," Johnny teased.

"And eat and sleep," Stefan added, laughing.

"Stefan thinks he's goin' to college," Johnny told Nate.

"I *will* go to college," Stefan corrected. "It will take many years, but I will go. You will see."

"Okay," Johnny said, rolling his eyes at Nate. He knelt to reach under a second bed, right beside Stefan's. The room had no other furniture. Johnny dragged out a box and rummaged around.

Stefan examined Nate. "*You* go to school, yes?"

"Yes."

"My brother, he talk about money, money," Stefan went on. Johnny came up with two old leather gloves, and Stefan turned to him: "How you will have money if you do not go to college? Hey? You will be breaker boss, Johnny, you think he is rich? You will be super, live in house at top of street? *That* is rich?"

Johnny said nothing, but he blushed.

"The only way a miner's son will ever get money is if he goes to college," Stefan finished, tapping his book. "Hey, Johnny? Someday, I go."

"I go, too," Johnny said, grabbing Nate's arm. "Come on, Nate."

Stefan chuckled and shook his head; Nate waved.

He hoped to get out before he had to meet anyone else, but when they reached the kitchen a woman entered, lugging two tin pails. She wore a heavy black skirt and a black blouse. Her feet were bare, and a kerchief was tied around her head, pulled nearly to her brow so that no hair showed. Was she Johnny's grandmother? Her eyes flashed over Nate from head to toe, and she began scolding Johnny in their language.

Johnny answered in a defiant tone. The only English word Nate heard was his own name as Johnny jerked a thumb toward him. He gestured to the berries, brandished the gloves. Then he poked his chest repeatedly, still talking, and Stefan called something down. The woman went to the stairwell and began to argue with him instead.

"Come on," Johnny mumbled, and they slipped out.

The bike had been left unattended. "That little . . ." Johnny said, looking around for Joey, but then he shrugged. "Oh well. Let's go." Whatever the reason for the argument, it hadn't upset him much. "Hey, Nate? Got any money?"

"No," Nate said right away, tensing up.

"Ah, that's awright. I got two nickels. Let's go to the store."

Nate felt ashamed as he walked his bicycle beside Johnny. How could he let a breaker boy spend money on him when he had a dollar in his pocket? But it was too late now. What could he say? *Oh, I forgot I had this.* Besides, if Johnny saw that dollar, he would be just like the town boys at school. Johnny would want Nate around for only one reason.

The company store was crowded and hot and loud with the confusion of foreigners talking, laughing, arguing. Children hung on women's skirts or darted about, playing tag. One woman examined a bolt of fabric, another held a cooking pot, and some stood in line.

A group of men gathered around a glass case that held cardboard boxes and tin cans in all shapes and sizes. There were picks and shovels, crowbars and lamps. Nate tugged on Johnny's arm. "What's all that stuff?"

"Powder. Squibs. Oil. Tools."

Nate gave him a questioning look.

"Mining supplies," Johnny explained.

"You mean they buy it themselves?"

"Yep. They get it here, and the company deducts it from their pay. Don't you know how the company store works, Nate?"

Nate knew the family owned the store, just as it owned the patch. Miners rented the patch houses, and they could buy whatever they needed right here, instead of having to walk all the way to Hazleton. But he never knew the miners had to buy their own work supplies.

He stuck close as Johnny made his purchases: a few pretzels and a root beer. Johnny handed over his nickels. Nate was surprised when no pennies were returned. "That's all you got?" he whispered as they left.

Johnny snorted. "They jack up all the prices."

"Why?" Nate asked, puzzled.

Turning from side to side, Johnny held out his arms. "Where else we gonna go?"

Nate looked around with new eyes. The patch, the breaker, and beyond that nothing but culm banks and woods and more breakers.

"Here." Johnny offered Nate a pretzel.

"No thanks," Nate said. "I'm not hungry."

And it wasn't a lie.

12

THE BASEBALL FIELD was scrubby, more dirt and weeds than grass, tucked away from the road over a rise. About fifteen boys were playing, but when Johnny and Nate appeared, they abandoned the game and swarmed them.

"Where he come from?"

"Who's the swell?"

"Where you been, Johnny?"

"Gimme a pretzel!"

"Izzat his bike?"

Some spoke English as well as Johnny, and some sounded like foreigners. They were dressed the way Johnny was, and all were barefoot. Nate felt foolish in his knee pants, high socks, and canvas shoes.

"That's Emil, and Anton," Johnny told Nate, pointing to the two biggest boys, who stood quietly behind the crowd. "This is Nate. Can he play?"

"He any good?" Anton asked.

Johnny shrugged. "I don't know, I just met him."

Anton questioned Nate with his eyes.

"Pretty good, I suppose," Nate said slowly.

"We'll see about that." Emil looked distrustful. "You take him," he told Anton.

"I guess I don't mind," Anton agreed.

Nate was put in the outfield on Johnny's team. Anton pitched, and Johnny caught for him. Anton threw fast; Nate was glad not to have to face him at bat. They didn't use a real baseball, but a hard rubber ball. Still, it must have hurt Johnny's hand to catch with that work glove.

Once, Anton's pitch hit a smaller boy named Mikey, who seemed to think it was no accident. He rushed at Anton, yelling in a foreign language, and soon both teams were brawling in a heap of thrashing arms and legs while Nate alone stayed out of it, watching, expecting disaster.

But after a while they got up, spat dirt, retrieved lost caps, and continued as if nothing had happened. Nate was amazed, because losing his temper the way Mikey did was just the sort of thing that always got *him* into trouble. Maybe he could get along with these boys. Maybe, if they thought he played well, they'd ask him back.

He tried his hardest—never struck out, and got three solid hits. Once he grounded to second, but ran fast even though it seemed a sure out. In right field, he scrambled for every ball that came his way, while taking care not to crowd the center fielder's territory. When he dived to make an inning-ending catch, Anton gave him an approving frown, nodding: "Not bad."

Anton's team won, 9–5. Then, as Nate tried to hide his surprise, the boys stretched out on the ground, pulling out cigarettes and plug tobacco. Even Fred and Tom didn't smoke, and they were sixteen and nineteen. How old *were* these boys, anyway? Some were surely younger than twelve. But then how could they work in the breaker?

Those who had no tobacco begged some from others until everyone had something to smoke or chew. Johnny took a bite off his plug, then offered it: "Want some, Nate?"

"Nah. No thanks," Nate mumbled.

"Where's he come from, anyway?" Emil asked Johnny.

"Whyncha ask him, Emil?" Johnny shot back. "He talks, I heard him with my own ears."

"Hazleton," Nate said.

Emil narrowed his eyes suspiciously. "Whatta you doin' over here?"

"Ridin' his bike, what's it look like?" Johnny said.

"Why you all dressed up?" one boy asked.

I'm not, Nate was about to say, but instead pretended he didn't hear the question.

"You rich boy?" someone said. "With bike like that?"

"Nah," Nate answered.

"His grandfather buys him stuff, Bobby," Johnny explained. "'Cause Nate's named after him. He's got a real baseball glove, too."

Nate squirmed with embarrassment, tugging at weeds.

"Where's your father work?" Emil's question sounded more like a challenge.

"At the electric company."

"He's a clerk," Johnny added.

"You got electricity in you house?" Bobby wanted to know.

"Um—yeah."

All except Emil expressed awe with a "Wow!" or a whistle or an intake of breath.

"You get it free?" Mikey asked.

"No, we pay for it. Just like everybody else." It was strange, all this talk of money and his father's job and what Nate did and did not have. Where he was from, people just did not ask about that sort of thing.

"You got real baseball at your home?" the littlest boy asked.

Before Nate could decide how to answer, Anton said, "Hey, next week's payday. Let's do a knockdown! Then we can buy a couple balls."

Most of the others agreed enthusiastically, though a boy named Andre needed persuading.

"What's a knockdown?" Nate asked Johnny, and the boys laughed.

"Well, see, when we go pick up our pay, we decide how much the knockdown's gonna be," Johnny explained. "Fifty cents, usually. Then we all take that much out before we give the pay to our mothers."

"That way everybody's pay's the same, so Mama doesn't figure it out," Anton added.

But Nate was puzzled. "I don't get it."

"Oh, Lee-dee-ah!" Johnny sang out in a high voice as he reached over to knock on Anton's head. "How much monny leetle Anton get heez pay thees time?"

"Oh, Irena, eez terrible!" Anton threw up his hands, mimicking his own mother. "Leetle Anton get only seex dollar!"

"Seex dollar! Same my Yonny!"

Catching on, Nate laughed along.

"Oh, eeeevil coal op-er-*ay*-tors!" Anton went on, and the boys howled.

"Hey, did you hear about this fellow John Fahy?" Emil asked, getting serious.

"Naw, whozzat?" Andre said.

"He's leader of this bunch called United Mine Workers. He's gonna bring all the miners together to fight for better pay. My father and my uncle were talkin' about it."

"Fight for *what*?" Mikey hooted.

"Who says?" Johnny added.

"Good luck!" Bobby jeered.

"It's true!" Emil protested. "They're doin' it in Pittsburgh and it can work here, too. But everybody's got to stick together and fight."

"You mean like the Mollies?" Johnny asked.

The very word made Nate shiver. Ever since he was little, he'd heard stories at school about the Molly Maguires, a group of Irish miners back in the '70s. They were so mad about the way things were, they formed a secret society to kill foremen and bosses, and to bomb collieries. When they were finally caught, they were hanged.

"Nothin' like the Mollies," Emil snapped. "They don't hurt anybody, they just get the miners together, and us fellows up top, too. It's called a union. And we all say, 'If you don't do this or that, we ain't gonna work.' If the operators don't want to get shut down, they gotta give in."

"That's bull," said Anton lazily. Everyone turned to him; he spat tobacco juice. "You know what a scab is, Emil? Mention *that* word to your father and uncle next time they talk about the union. See what they say then."

Nobody spoke until Nate asked quietly, "What's a scab?"

"Scabs are the workers who won't go on strike. Or new ones the operators bring in—like maybe all the Dagos just come over, kickin' around Lattimer, lookin' for work. Last time there was a strike, his father was a scab, and his, and his"—Anton pointed out each boy, and each in turn looked at the ground—"and mine," Anton finished, defiantly jabbing his own chest. "They did it because they had to put food on the table. But my old man ain't proud of it. So think about *that* when you hear talk about strikes and unions and Fahy. We strike, there goes our jobs."

Nate was miserable and didn't know where to look. As usual, he'd gotten himself into an impossible situation. He should not be hearing this. Then again, surely his family knew it already. *The good Lord knows there's trouble enough brewing at the collieries.* Of course, this must be what Grandpa had meant.

"Aw, forget it," Mikey said, shambling to his feet. "Nate? Can I try your bike?"

Others joined in. "Yeah, Nate."

"Can we?"

"We'll be careful."

"Please?"

"Sure," he said.

They cheered and ran off, leaving Nate with Johnny, Anton, and Emil. "Anybody want to see the cockfights?" Anton asked, getting up.

"I'll go," Emil said grudgingly.

"Johnny?" Anton said.

"Naw. Papa says I can't," Johnny muttered.

"Oh, wittle Yonny!" Anton grabbed a handful of Johnny's shiny, straight black hair, laughing.

Johnny gave a good-natured scowl.

"See you, then," Anton said. "Good game, Nate."

"Thanks."

"See you, Johnny," Emil said.

"So long." Johnny leaned up on his elbow, studying Nate. "Hey, maybe you can bring your friends sometime, and we can play against you." He grinned. "If your friends ain't afraid to play with a bunch of Hunkies."

The offer caught Nate off guard, but he thought—and lied—fast. "I don't really know anybody else around here."

"How come?"

"I— We just moved here a couple weeks ago."

"You did? How come you didn't say?"

Nate shrugged, forcing a smile. "You didn't ask."

"Well, where'd you move from?"

Somewhere familiar, nearby, similar: "Mauch Chunk."

"Oh yeah? I went to Mauch Chunk once. It's nice there, ain't it?"

Nate nodded.

"I like the river."

"Yeah, I'll miss the Lehigh," Nate said wistfully.

They sat in silence a while, then Johnny said, "Well, you can play with us again, if you want. If Anton says 'good game,' it means you can play again. Want to?"

Nate shrugged. "Sure."

"We play every day after work," Johnny said.

Nate's heart fell. He had forgotten: all afternoon, while he was moping around bored, they'd be together in the breaker. They were so lucky to have one another, running wild, playing together when they weren't at work, conspiring on things like this knockdown.

"Right about five-thirty," Johnny continued, interrupting Nate's thoughts. "First we gotta go home and get a bath, then we come back out. You gotta run around, after sittin' all day. We play about an hour, till supper."

Nate did the arithmetic. If he left home at five, he'd arrive at the field when they did. If they stopped at six-thirty, he'd make it back just in time for dinner . . .

"Usually it's Emil's team against Anton's," Johnny was saying. "But sometimes we put both teams together and play against another breaker, like Banbury or Lattimer."

"Oh," Nate said distractedly.

"You know who's good? The Dagos over at Lattimer. Who taught a buncha Italians to play baseball so good, I wanna know! Some of those fellas only been here a year or two!"

"Uh-huh," Nate said. He would have to explain his absence every day. And what if he passed relatives on the road, going to or from one of the collieries? Well, he would figure it out. Because he *was* going to play baseball.

"So, Nate, you think you'll come?"

"All right," Nate said. "Sure."

Johnny checked him over. "How old are you, anyway?"

"Twelve."

"Same with me! Well, almost. I'll *be* twelve. Next month."

"I thought—" Nate cut himself off.

"What?"

"I heard somewhere you had to be twelve to work in a breaker."

"Well, that's the law." He winked, grinning. "But I been almost two years in the breaker now."

"Two *years!*" Nate nearly shouted.

"Sure. I was ten when I went in. Luka? The little fella? He's nine. He came in a few weeks ago."

"But why?" Nate asked, mystified.

Johnny made a fist, rubbing his index finger against his thumb. "Money. A family can't get ahead on a miner's wages. Mama and Papa are saving to buy a house. And they send money back to Poland for my grandparents. So me and my brother, we help. Next year, maybe, Joey comes to the breaker, too. And we got a boarder, from our town in Poland."

"You do? Where's he sleep?"

"With me. Joey sleeps with Stefan."

"Oh. So it's Poland you're from?"

"Well, not me. *I'm* from right here," Johnny said proudly.

"Stefan, he was born in Poland. Papa came alone, at first. After he saved enough money, he sent for Mama and Stefan. When Mama and Papa got back together, they had me." Johnny winked knowingly, and Nate felt his face redden.

"So that's why your English is better than Stefan's. You were born here."

"Yeah. I talk American, but Stefan's a lot smarter than me. He reads all the time. Even down below on lunch break, usin' his miner's lamp."

"How old's Stefan?"

"Seventeen."

"How long's he been underground?"

"Oh, since he was about thirteen. He was a nipper."

"What's that?"

"Nipper?" Johnny shook his head. "That's the worst job of all. You sit by the doors all day, alone in the dark, listenin' for the stable boys bringin' the coal cars. When you hear 'em comin', you got to jump up real fast to open the doors. If you ain't fast enough, the cars crash into the doors and you could be killed."

Boys did such work? Boys just a little older than he was? Nate scratched at the dirt with a stick. The breaker didn't seem so bad, but sitting in the dark, getting killed by coal cars? Could it be true?

"Stefan didn't mind it, though," Johnny went on. "He just did more readin'. But now he's a butty. You know what a butty is, don't you?"

"Yeah," Nate said. The butty was the miner's helper, who did most of the hard and dirty work. The two went together

66

to their underground chamber, and the miner told the butty where to blast. And when the miner felt like leaving for the day, he just left his butty to finish loading the coal alone. It was the butties who had the tough job, that was what Nate heard. The miners pretty much did as they pleased. They never listened to the supervisors. They even made a show of *not* working when the supervisors were around.

"Too bad Stefan can't be Papa's butty," Johnny said. "The company don't allow it, fathers and sons workin' together."

"How come?"

Johnny shrugged. "They're just mean. But it don't matter. One day, Stefan'll be a miner with papers. Then *he'll* be givin' the orders to *his* butty."

"But Stefan said he's going to college."

"Stefan dreams." Johnny smiled indulgently, shaking his head. "But he's a good brother. Before, at my house? Mama wanted me to haul water, and he was tellin' Mama to let me go out and have some fun."

"So that was your mother?"

Johnny gave him a quizzical look. "Who'd you *think* it was?"

Nate shrugged, hoping Johnny didn't notice him blushing.

"You got any brothers or sisters?" Johnny asked.

"Yeah. Two older brothers, one older sister, and two little sisters, they're twins. And two more, they're sort of my brothers, but not really."

"What's that mean?" Johnny asked with a funny look.

"I have a stepmother," Nate mumbled. "They're her sons."

"Your mama die?"

Nate nodded.

"When?"

"When I was seven."

"Your stepma—her boys' papa died?"

"No. My pa's their father."

"Well, then they *are* your brothers."

"I suppose." He quickly changed the subject. "Did you ever go to school?"

"Sure I did! Four years! I can read and write okay. That's all I need. And if the company would give us better pay, and not make us buy at the company store, I—"

"*Make* you?"

"Yeah. If we don't, we maybe lose our jobs. And they don't play fair by us. Papa says he can get his powder in town much cheaper than they charge. And food, Mama can buy eggs and flour in Hazleton about half what it costs at Harland. But we almost never get up to town. And besides, they keep track. If you don't buy at the store, they want to know why."

"That isn't fair!" Nate protested.

Johnny shrugged. "Well, we're used to it. But I guess this guy Fahy's tryin' to change it."

"Yeah," Nate mumbled. He felt hot and sick and thirsty. He should have stayed in town. Begged his stupid cousin to let him play, if baseball was so important. He had no business among the breaker boys; he was everything they hated. And he was an impostor. "I should go," he said, getting to his feet.

Johnny stood, too, and stuck out his hand. "It's good we met." He flashed a grin that lit his face and his black eyes. "Don't you think?"

"Uh, yeah," Nate stammered. "But I've got to get going." He walked quickly toward the road.

"Hey, Nate?" Johnny called, and he turned. "Monday?" Nate shrugged. "Okay."

Never go back, he warned himself on the ride home. If Pa knew what he'd been up to . . . Nate shuddered. Pa had never spelled it out: *Do not play with miners' boys.* But that was only because he didn't think he had to. The miners had their own towns, their own friends, their own churches—even their own religion, Catholic, just like the Irish miners before them. The miners' families stayed together, and the operators' families stayed together. That was just the way it was.

But Johnny had been nicer to Nate than any boy he could remember. Here, where no one knew him, he could become a whole new person. Nate thought again of the dollar in his pocket, of Johnny saying *Ah, that's awright. I got two nickels.* Nate hadn't told them he had a baseball, but that would have made no difference, either. Next time, Nate told himself, I'll bring one of my baseballs.

Next time! Yes, he *would* come back again, and again and again if they'd let him. If Pa found out, what of it? Surely he was already planning to send Nate off to another boarding school. What more could he do? Thrash him? Lock him in his room? It would be worth it, just to have a friend.

A friend.

Nate laughed as he zigzagged along the road. He had a friend.

13

NATE TAPPED AT his brother's open door. "Tom?"

"Hello, Nathan." Tom stood before the mirror, pomading his hair. "What's up?"

"Oh, nothing," Nate said, swinging on the door.

"Come in."

Nate leaned against the wall beside Tom's bureau. "That stuff stinks."

Tom laughed. "You certainly do have an ingratiating way about you. But I'll have you know there's a certain young lady who quite likes the stink of this stuff."

"Alice Parker?" Nate asked, twisting his mouth. *"Still?"*

"I'll tell you a secret, Nate," Tom said with a wink. "She'll be my bride before the century turns."

"The century! That's ages away!"

"Only two and a half years. And you know what you'll find? The older you get, the faster time flies."

"Hmm," Nate said. Tom sure was spending enough time on that hair, placing every wave. As bad as a girl.

"So, what's on your mind? It's unlike you to come around for a chat."

"Oh, I was just wondering about something."

"And what might that be?"

"Well, it's Grandpa. He said something peculiar to me."

"Nate, Grandpa's *always* saying something peculiar," Tom replied, chuckling.

"No, this was different. He said trouble was brewing at the collieries. What do you suppose he meant by that?"

Somber at once, Tom put the brush down. "*Grandpa* said that to *you*?"

Nate nodded. "He didn't mean to. You know how sometimes he says things . . . not really *to* you."

"I worked for Grandpa an entire summer," Tom said with a wry grin. "I know."

"Anyhow, what did he mean?"

"Nate"—Tom reached out to ruffle his hair—"it's nothing for you to fret over."

"I'm not fretting!" Nate protested. "I just want to know! Pa says I'm not a child anymore, but everybody treats me like one."

"All right." Tom sat on his bed and patted the spot beside him. "This is between us, right?"

Nate sat. "Right."

"Do you know what a union is, Nathan?"

If he played dumb, he might learn more. "Um, an army?"

Tom laughed. "Good one! A union is when workers band together to squeeze their employer for more money. It's happening in Pittsburgh—not here, not yet. But Grandpa and Pa and Uncle Henry and Uncle George and all the other coal operators are worried that our workers will organize, too. That's the term for it, organizing. Understand?"

Nate nodded. "But why are they worried?"

"Because they don't want a strike. You know what a strike is, don't you?"

"'Course I do. But if they don't want a strike, couldn't they just give the miners what they want?"

"Well, they *could*," Tom said. "But Grandpa refuses to deal with the union, Nate. He says it would be like giving in to a kidnapper's threats. It's holding the company hostage, that's what unionizing is. And if we gave in, they might think 'Hey, that was easy! Let's do it again!' Do you understand, Nate?"

"I suppose."

"And besides, the truth of it is, we just don't have that much to give."

"What do you mean?"

"Mining coal's not as profitable as it once was, Nate. What the miners don't understand is that we're fighting for our *own* survival these days."

"We are?" Nate asked. "Who are we fighting?"

"The railroads. They control how we get our coal to market, and they're owned by extremely rich men."

"We're rich," Nate mumbled.

Tom smiled indulgently. "We're rich in Hazleton, Nathan. I'm talking about Philadelphia rich, New York rich. Those people dictate when we can ship coal, how much we can ship at a time, and how much we have to pay to ship it. And it's never enough for them. They always want more. They want our companies, too."

"They do?" Nate asked, frowning.

"Yes, they do. They're perched like vultures on a fence, just waiting for us to fail so they can swoop down and gobble us up. They'll be able to do it, too, if we have to give away our remaining profits to these whining miners."

"Then what would happen? Would we be poor?"

"Well, we wouldn't be poor, exactly, but"—he shrugged—"things could change."

"What things?"

"Oh, don't worry." Tom got to his feet, switching off the light. "It'll all blow over. You'll see." He patted Nate's shoulder. "I've got to be off, Nate. Remember, don't let Pa know I spoke to you about this. I don't think he'd like it."

Alone in his room, Nate pondered his brother's words: *Holding the company hostage.* If that was really what unions did, it wasn't fair. But what of the company store? And Nate had seen Johnny's house, a company house. He couldn't tell Tom that. *Things could change . . .*

The family was mad about the union, and scared of being shut down. The miners were scared of losing their jobs, but mad about their pay and about the company store. And the railroad companies were waiting like vultures on a fence.

Nate dug into his wardrobe and pulled out the wooden box. He lay on the floor and lined up his soldiers, the blue against the gray.

14

ON MONDAY Nate scoured the trunk room, rummaging through the worn and outgrown clothes Fiona collected for the Catholic missions. Maybe he could wear this torn shirt of Patrick's with the sleeves rolled. And if he cut the bands from Fred's old knee pants, he'd have long pants that were too short for his legs—just like the breaker boys'.

Perhaps he should go shoeless, too. Stripping off his socks, he poked at his tender soles. If he tried to run barefoot on that scrubby field . . . He pictured himself bouncing on tip-toe, wincing with discomfort. No, he couldn't pull it off. Besides, one look at these white toes and the boys would know that his feet rarely saw daylight.

Finally he decided to leave his appearance alone. It was bad enough that he was pretending to be someone else. He ought at least to *look* like the person he was. The boys knew he lived in town. They would have to accept his canvas shoes and knee pants.

But as he rode toward the field, his confidence blew away with the breeze. Saturday seemed ages ago. What if Johnny forgot that he'd asked Nate to return? Even worse: What if he regretted asking? What if the others disagreed, and drove him away? But he must find out. If he backed down now, he'd hate himself for not even trying.

Nate was dizzy with anxiety as he got off his bike. The boys were calling to one another, laughing, shouting. When Nate reached the crest of the rise, all action seemed to freeze as everyone looked at him—puzzled, expectant, critical. Nate stifled the urge to show them the baseball tucked in his glove. Would they welcome him for himself? He knew he was about to find out.

Then Johnny waved like a windmill, calling, "Come on!" Nate threw the ball and ran to join him.

From then on, the breaker whistle was a new noise, signaling fun and freedom after a dull day. The mornings were all right: Mr. Hawthorne wasn't quite so boring as other teachers. But the afternoons were endless and agonizing, beginning with the lunchtime inquisition.

Every day, Pa asked, *What plans have you for the afternoon, Nate?* Nate would try to sound casual, uncaring, but his response always came out high and strained: *Ohhh, nothing.* Then Pa would spout off about how he didn't understand why Nate couldn't play with George and the others. Once he announced, right in front of everybody, that Will's parents had taken George and eight other boys to Mauch Chunk on the train for Will's birthday.

Every day, Nate left the dining room angry and morose. Why couldn't he be more like Tory? She was always cheerful and content. Often she played house with the twins, using Anna's boys as real-life dolls. Sometimes they played school, which annoyed Nate no end: Why did girls want to *pretend* to be in a classroom? Didn't they get enough of the real thing?

When she wasn't with the children, Tory spent hours reading on the porch swing, until Anna gently scolded her: *You always have your nose in a book!* Nate would have fumed at such intrusions, but Tory just laughed and went off to play tennis or call on a friend, occasionally asking Nate to come along.

She was only being polite, and he had no interest in sipping tea on some girl's lawn, or watching as they curled their hair, or whatever girls got up to. He declined her invitations and hung around the grounds, taking off as soon as he heard the whistle.

Then, one afternoon, Anna waylaid him as he was about to leave. "You've been spending a great deal of time out riding, Nate," she said cheerfully.

"Uh-huh," he answered.

"Do you use the bicycle paths at Hazle Park?"

"Sometimes," he lied, and she asked nothing else. But it made him realize that she was keeping an eye on him—and that if she connected his departure with the breaker whistle, he was doomed.

So he started to leave the grounds at various times. He rowed in the Hazle Park lake or visited the kinetoscope parlor, where he slid nickels into the machines and watched a few seconds of moving pictures: a circus, a rodeo, a prizefight. Sometimes he went early to the baseball field, throwing himself pop flies while waiting for his new friends.

At first all the breaker boys, except for Johnny and Anton and Emil, looked the same to Nate, but each day he got to know someone else a little better.

Scrappy little Mikey was scared of nobody. He loved stealing bases, fearlessly charging anyone who dared to block him. He was the oldest of eight; his father, Johnny said, liked his liquor too much, and drank most of his pay.

Andre was quiet and a little shy, but a determined ballplayer whose at bat prompted Anton to shout "Move back!" to his fielders. Andre was more serious than the others, probably because his father had been killed two years ago in a fall of coal. So Andre was the man of the house. He was always the last to agree to a knockdown, because he knew how much his mother needed his pay.

Bobby had come from Poland only two years ago, but had quickly learned to fit in. When the others teased him about his broken English and thick accent, he just laughed. He was brash and outspoken, chattering in the field as loud as anybody.

Luka was a sort of mascot, everybody's little brother. At play, they made him fetch the ball; at work, they made him fetch everything. Johnny said Luka's mother complained that the boys were teaching him bad habits: smoking, swearing, lying. The other mothers only shrugged and said it was to be expected when you sent your son into the breaker.

Johnny seemed to be everybody's favorite—which made Nate wonder all the more why Johnny liked *him*. He always rushed to Nate when he saw him, and when their team was at bat they sat together in the weeds, talking. Johnny liked to entertain him with stories about the breaker: the tricks they played on the boss, who loomed over them with his stick; the way they'd throw slate into the machinery, jamming it so they could have a rest; the lunchtime wars, with screws and nuts as ammunition. Nate listened and laughed and asked questions, but rarely talked about himself. When Johnny asked about school or his family, or about what he did all day, Nate answered as briefly as possible. He was forever on guard, worried that he might slip and say something about his family. Always on his mind were the words *impostor, fake.* Always he expected to be found out.

One day the breaker boys arrived with bottles of root beer and a sack full of candy. "Nate!" Johnny held out a bottle. "We're celebratin'!"

"Oh, yeah?" Nate asked, taking it. "Celebrating what?"

"It's Anton! He got promoted to spragger!"

Anton nodded proudly.

"To whatter?" Nate asked, and everybody laughed.

Mikey passed him the candy. "Don't you know nothin'?"

"No." Nate yanked Mikey's cap over his eyes. "I don't. So tell me."

"Spraggers stop the coal cars comin' down the tracks," Johnny explained.

"Stop them how?" Nate said.

"By stickin' a sprag in the wheel."

"What's a sprag?" Nate asked, and they howled.

Anton jumped up, brandishing a stick. "Sprag is like this, only bigger. You run next to the car, then you jab the sprag in at just the right spot, and it stops the car." Anton demonstrated, running along, bending way over to poke his stick at an imaginary wheel.

"You got to be *fast* to be a spragger," Johnny said, nodding in admiration. "It's the life, though, ain't it, Anton?"

"No more breaker boss," Anton agreed. "No more back-breakin' slate-pickin'." He tapped his chest. "I'm underground now."

"Yeah, and soon he won't want to play ball with the likes of us," Johnny teased.

"Sure I will!"

"We'll see about that," Emil replied with a sly nod, and Mikey jumped on Anton's back, playfully pulling off his cap, as a group circled to tug on Anton's arms.

Nate took a nickel from his pocket and offered it to Johnny. "What's that?"

"Give it to whoever bought the root beer and the candy."

"No, no, no," Johnny said, holding up his hands. "It's on me."

Nate already knew better than to argue. As long as Johnny had a penny in his pocket, he would spend it on someone else. "Thanks," Nate said. "So, is that what you want to do next? Be a spragger?"

"Not me! But I can't wait till I get down below. I want to be a mule driver."

"Yeah? When'll that be?"

"Well, you don't get to be a driver right off. First you're a stable boy—you take care of the mules."

Nate made a face. "You'd *like* that?"

"Oh, yeah, I love those poor animals. They have to spend their whole lives underground. But they can be real nice, if you know how to treat 'em. See, if you're mean to them, they'll be mean to you. Kick you so hard they'll break your leg. Maybe even kill you. But if you're good to them, they'll be good to you. And if you're a good stable boy, then you get promoted to driver."

"And *that's* the real life," Anton added.

"Oh, yeah," Mikey agreed.

"I want to be stable boy, too," Bobby said.

"Wait in line, greenhorn," Johnny taunted him.

Nate had to wonder: how many would actually get this dream job?

"Sing Nate the song, Johnny," Mikey said.

"Awww, *you* sing it."

"You! You do it best," Mikey urged, and the others took up the plea.

"Go on, Johnny," Anton said. "It's my promotion, I want to hear *you* sing it."

"Ahh, all right." Johnny scowled, but he was grinning. He bit a hunk off his plug as the boys waited for the performance. Johnny stood and cleared his throat, stretching his arms dramatically and singing in a loud warble:

"My sweetheart's the mule in the mines
I drive her without reins or lines
On the bumper I sit
I chew and I spit
All over my sweetheart's behind!"

At the word "spit" he turned his head to demonstrate, shooting tobacco juice through his teeth and returning to the tune without missing a beat.

The boys laughed and cheered as if they'd never heard it before—Nate twice as hard because he hadn't.

Johnny bowed to the right and the left. "Thank you. Thank you, one and all!"

"Okay," Anton finally said, getting to his feet. "Who came here to play ball?"

As everyone jumped up and headed for the field, Anton took hold of Nate's arm. "Hey." Nate turned to him. "I been watchin' you." Nate frowned; Anton grinned. "You're pretty good, you know?"

"Thanks," Nate mumbled, breathing a sigh of relief.

"What's your best position?"

"Third base."

Anton nodded. "Bobby—shortstop!" he called out. "Luka—right!" He gave Nate a little push: "Third base."

15

"Oh, Nathan!" Mary sang out as he started down the porch stairs. "Where y' off to now?"

"Out."

She was sitting at the other end of the porch with a colander in her lap, snapping the ends off string beans. "I need a favor."

"What?" He cast a suspicious look at Anna's little boys,

who were playing on the floor. This favor had better not have anything to do with them.

"Mrs. Tanner's due back at any moment." Mary was already up and untying her apron strings. "And I've *got* to rush into town before the meat market closes."

"Oh, no . . ." Nate shook his head, backing away.

"Some of the chops are spoiled. I must get back or there'll not be enough dinner."

Nate glanced at the boys: Martin was building with blocks, James climbing onto a chair. It was Lucy's day off. "Why can't Fiona see to them?" he asked.

"Fiona's down with a headache. Oh, Nate, be a dear. Mrs. Tanner will return from her tea any time now."

"Well . . . what do I have to do?" he grumbled.

"Just *watch* them. Very closely. Make sure they don't climb on things."

"You mean like that one?" he asked, pointing.

"Oh!" Mary rushed over and lifted James from the chair. " 'That one' happens to be named James," she said indignantly, holding him toward Nate.

"Ahh!" he yelped, jumping back. "I'm not going to *touch* it!"

She eyed him fiercely. "Well, just watch them, would y'?" she said, putting the boy on the floor.

"Well, make it snappy, would *you*?" he replied.

"That mouth o' yours, Nathan." She clucked as she descended the steps. "Honestly, I . . ."

"Over there." Nate nudged James with his toe. "Go over there with the other one." James crawled across the porch.

They were a foolish-looking pair of children, with their golden ringlets and silly puffy outfits. They hardly even looked like boys. Nate supposed it was natural for women and girls to fuss over them, but why did Pa turn into an imbecile when they were around? Singing ridiculous songs, creeping on all fours, letting them pull his nose—in general, not behaving like Pa at all.

"All right." Nate sat on the glider. "Now you play with him," he said to Martin, pointing to James.

"No!" Martin protected his block tower with his arms. "He bweak it, Nayfin!"

Nate stared in shock. When had this one learned to talk? Even more surprising, it sounded as if Martin had said his name. But was that possible? He leaned forward and asked quietly, "*What's* my name?"

"Nayfin."

"Right. And you're, uh, James, aren't you?" Nate slid to the floor.

"No!" he giggled. "I Mottin!"

"Oh, yeah, Martin. So, um, he breaks your stuff? Your little brother?" He began to help Martin build.

"He bweak my bwocks. Evwy time!"

"You know the twins? Millie and Winnie, you know them?"

Martin nodded, wide-eyed.

"When I was little, they'd always knock over my toy soldiers when I had them set up. It made me mad."

"I hab sojers."

"You do?"

"Mama gabe me sojers."

"Oh yeah? My mother gave me—" Nate stopped. *Mine for my seventh birthday.* But just a few days later, Mama was confined; Nate didn't even get his kiss before school. She and Nate had hoped for a boy, because he was surrounded by sisters. But when he returned that afternoon, both she and his baby brother were dead.

"Anyway," Nate said, stacking blocks. "How old are you?"

"I fwee."

"You *are*? When did that happen?"

"I doe know."

"So, how old's your brother? Two?"

"I doe know. We biwd a big cassew, Nayfin!"

"A what? Oh, yeah, a castle."

Just then a shadow fell on them, and Martin yelled "Nooo!"

As James lurched forward, Nathan swung his arm back to fend him off, protecting Martin's tower. But the baby went sprawling and set up a wail.

At that unfortunate moment, Anna swept up the porch steps. "Oh! Darling!" she gasped, scooping up her howling son. "Oh! Nathan, what's happened?"

"Nayfin push him," Martin said.

"I didn't!" Nate protested. He whirled on Martin: "You treacherous little brat!"

Martin cowered and began to cry.

"Oh, Nate, how *could* you!" Anna looked as if she might start blubbering right along with them. She knelt to gather Martin in her arms, too.

"Well, this is fine, just fine!" Nate stomped to the porch steps. "This is the last time I do a favor for a *servant!*"

"*Nathan!*" Anna said sharply.

"Next time, look after your own brats," he shot back. "Oh, I forgot—*you* married a rich man. You don't *have* to look after children anymore."

Anna's eyes went wide with horror. Her mouth flew open, but no sound came out. She scrambled to her feet and started for him. "Nathan, you apologize *this very instant!*" she demanded as he jumped down the steps. "Nathan!" she called tearfully.

He did not turn around.

Anton's team was in position when Nate jogged over the rise.

"You're late!" Anton yelled.

Nate didn't answer. He tossed Johnny the ball, muttering "Hi."

Johnny frowned. "Whatsa matter, Nate?"

"Huh?"

"You look mad."

Nate shook his head and started for third base.

"Play ball!" Anton called.

But Nate couldn't stop thinking about the scene on the porch. Why couldn't he have held his temper and tried to explain, instead of getting himself into trouble again? Yet Anna had been so ready to blame him, without even asking what happened.

The innings crept past. Time and again, Johnny asked what was wrong. Nate kept saying it was nothing.

The game went on longer than usual, and the score was 7–7 in the last of the six innings they played. Emil was on second with two outs when Nate let an easy grounder glance off his shin. Emil's team shouted "Score! Score!" as Emil whizzed past Nate. He fired the ball to Johnny, but it sailed over Johnny's head. Emil crossed home with a showy laziness, winning the game.

Anton threw down his glove in disgust.

"Whatta you doin'?" Luka yelled. "Watchin' flowers grow?"

"Shut up!" Nate shouted back. "Just shut up and let me be!" He stalked over to Johnny and held out his hand. "Give it!"

Johnny dropped the ball into his glove; Emil stood by, snickering.

"Aww, the leetle girly go home!" Bobby called.

"Who needs your damn ball?" Mikey yelled.

Nate and Johnny looked at each other. Nate returned the ball and stormed off the field. But when he was near his bike, he heard running behind him.

"Nate!"

"What?" Nate turned fast, spoiling for a fight.

Johnny shrugged. "I'll ask you once more. Whatsa matter?"

"Ahhh . . ." Nate kicked at the dirt. "Johnny, can I sleep at your house tonight?"

"My house!" Johnny clapped his hands to his chest, laughing. "Nate, you saw my house! Where we gonna put you?"

"I could sleep on the floor," Nate mumbled.

"You and the rats?"

"Rats?"

Johnny waved his hand, shook his head. "You in trouble?"

Of course he couldn't tell a story that began "Our cook asked me to watch my stepmother's boys." So he chose his words carefully: "I had an argument with my stepmother. I was looking after her boys, and I knocked one of them down by accident. She blamed me and I got mad and called them brats. And told her to take care of them herself next time."

Even without the remarks about favors for servants and Anna marrying a rich man, it sounded pretty bad.

"Go home, Nate," Johnny said, slapping his back. "When you're in a fix like that, nothing to do but face up to it."

"I suppose."

"Your pa the beatin' kind?"

"On occasion."

"Well, take it like a man, I say. 'Cause if you'll ever get beat, it'll be tonight," Johnny said cheerfully.

"I guess."

"Hey," Johnny said as Nate got on his bike. "If you're still alive tomorrow, or if you can walk, come to the swimming hole near the patch around two o'clock."

"Why?" Nate was puzzled: Who would be there then?

"We're gonna walk out. Our boss is gettin' too high and mighty, and we're sick of it." Johnny was grinning devilishly. "We'll shut the whole colliery down, see how they like *that*!"

Could it be true that they were able to shut down the colliery? Nate was in awe: They had such power, out in the world, working like men. And he was still a child, under Pa's thumb, obliged to him for everything.

"Hey, Nate!" Johnny tossed the baseball.

Nate threw it back right away. "You hang on to it."

"You givin' it to me in your will? Like after your father kills you?"

Nate had to laugh then.

"So you'll come swimming?" Johnny asked again.

"Oh, I don't know," Nate muttered, feeling his face burn. "Everybody's mad at me."

"Phhh," Johnny said, waving him off. "They forgot about it already." He punched Nate's arm. "See you tomorrow!" he called as he ran.

16

NATE CREPT INTO THE KITCHEN just as Mary bustled through the pantry's swinging doors. Her eyes shot fire, and she advanced on him, hissing, "I'd strangle y' if y' were mine, I swear I would! Y' made her cry, y' did, and I hope y're proud of y'rself, young man. Now y're late to dinner and y'r da's askin' for y'. Wash y'r hands right here and get in there!"

Nate was so dispirited, he couldn't work up the energy for backtalk. As he lathered his hands in the sink, Mary lingered with a towel, murmuring, "Imagine, speakin' to her like that. She does her best by y'. For shame, Nathan, for shame."

"Leave it, Mary," he said at last, and bravely headed for the dining room.

Pa's back was to him. It was Anna's pale, sorrowful face that he saw first. She glanced at him quickly, then averted her eyes. Nate waited for Pa's level, angry words. But as he walked to his seat, Pa only said, "The late Nate Tanner," in a tolerant, even jovial, voice.

Nate pulled in his chair and picked up his napkin. "Sorry." He cleared his throat. What was Pa's game tonight? Cat and mouse?

"Are you doing centuries on that bicycle every day, Nathan?" Pa asked.

Tom, Fred, and Tory laughed. Centuries were all the talk lately—one-hundred-mile bicycle rides had become a popular pastime. When Pa's joke failed to amuse Anna, he asked, "Dear, is anything wrong? You don't seem yourself this evening."

Nate was shocked to numbness. *Anna had not told Pa!*

She worked up a smile. "No, dear, I'm fine. I'm just a little under the weather, I suppose."

Pa's face creased into a worried frown. "Should you go up to bed, Anna?" he asked, starting to rise.

"No, no, Thomas. Sit, please. I'm fine, truly. I'll just have an early bed. A bit off par, that's all." To prove nothing was wrong, she picked up her fork and took a bite of lamb. "Mmm. Perfectly cooked, isn't it?"

"Wonderful, wonderful," Pa agreed.

After dinner, Tory asked Nate to walk to Jacobs' for ice cream with her and the twins. But he said he was tired and went to his room. He sat on the bed, feeling miserable, feeling as if something had been left undone. Pa had been so cheerfully ignorant. Better a thrashing than this peculiar sense of shame.

All at once the door flew open and Fred barged in.

"Hey!" Nate protested.

Fred grabbed his hair, forcing him to his feet. "What've you done now?"

"Let go!" Nate swung at him, and Fred caught his arm and twisted it behind his back.

"I know you did something." Fred's punch in the stomach nearly took Nate's breath away. "I could tell by your ugly face." Fred drilled his ribs, and Nate cried out without meaning to. "Shut up." Fred covered Nate's mouth and pulled him to the floor, pummeling him. Fred never hit him in the face, never left a telltale bruise. And Nate never bit the hand that silenced him. He had tried it once, but the beating that followed left him knowing better than to defend himself again.

Nate struggled to his feet the moment Fred got up. He wouldn't give Fred the satisfaction of staying on the floor. But he felt he might collapse as he choked out, "Get . . . out . . . of . . . my . . . room."

"You're a troublemaker, Nathan," Fred spat. "You don't belong in this family. I can't wait till Pa sends you to England." He stomped out of the room.

England! Nate fell onto the bed, holding his stomach. He'd heard about English boarding schools—they made Brock seem like paradise. He had been behaving. Pa didn't know about today. Yet Pa was planning to send him to England? How could Pa have pretended to joke with him at dinner? Did Tory know? Wouldn't she stand up for him? Wouldn't anybody? He hugged a pillow to his aching ribs, wishing he were on Johnny's floor with the rats.

Two sharp knocks at the door. He forced himself to an uncomfortable sitting position and said, "Come in."

Anna swept across the room and began to fuss with the draperies. "Martin was able to explain what happened, after you left," she said, undoing the tiebacks. "I misunderstood; for that I apologize." She moved to the next window. "But you could have told me yourself, Nathan, could you not?" She turned to him. "Could you not?"

"Everybody's always ready to blame me for—"

"No." She interrupted him coldly. "*You* are always ready, Nathan. Always ready to fight. Always ready to push me away. Haven't I tried, Nate? Haven't I?" she asked, her voice quavering. He did not answer. "I am sorry your mother died, Nathan, but I can't bring her back." Now tears spilled down her cheeks. She brushed them quickly away. "And I am sorry that you cannot accept Martin and James as your brothers, but they *are*. And you hurt Martin's feelings so badly. That's the part I—" She spun away and spent far too much time closing the rest of the draperies.

Nate stared at the bedspread, gulping down his feelings until she faced him again.

"There's one thing I wish to make perfectly clear." Her

voice was now icy and controlled. "I married your father for one reason: love. I expect *never* to have to remind you of that again. And I promise you, Nathan, there will be a day of reckoning if you ever again speak to me as you did this afternoon."

When her hand was on the doorknob, Nate said, "Anna?" She stopped.

"I won't," he told her. "And . . ." He looked down at his hands, gripping the edge of the bed so tightly that his knuckles were white. Then he raised his eyes to hers and pushed out the words. "I'm sorry."

Anna lifted her chin, turned her head, and closed the door softly behind her.

17

NATE HADN'T GONE SWIMMING once this summer, due to Pa's ironclad rule: No swimming alone, ever, under any circumstances. When Pa was a boy, his older brother, age eleven, failed to come home one summer evening. His clothing was found by a swimming hole, and Grandpa had to get leave from the war. Pa said it was the only time in his life he had ever seen his father cry. The story had made a grave impression on Nate—not because Pa would ever cry for him, but because drowning seemed a horrible death.

Even on the hottest days, when he was sorely tempted, it was the one rule he never broke.

In the brush between the Harland colliery and patch, he waited by the swimming hole. The boys should be here soon—if this thing really was going to happen. Maybe it was just Johnny's wishful thinking.

Nate never swam without a bathing suit, but he knew not to bring one today. Still, he felt uneasy. What would it be like, everyone running around in the nude? He surely would be embarrassed—and they surely would not be.

The breaker machinery moaned into silence. Seconds later there were shrieks and war whoops, the clatter of hobnail boots, and the shout "Come back here, you hoodlums!" from the Irish breaker boss.

And then the boys broke through the trees, laughing, yelling, unlacing and kicking away their boots as they ran, peeling off their clothes, their bodies glaringly white compared to their coal-blackened faces and hands. Nate watched, gleeful. It was like looking through a kinetoscope at someone else's daring, exciting life.

"Did you see the way he—"

"I got him right in the—"

"That was great, how you—"

Voices jumbled together as the boys recounted their exploits. Into the swimming hole they leaped, by ones and twos, calling "Hurry! Hurry!"

"You're alive!" Johnny yelled, splashing him. "Come on in!"

Nate took a furtive look around. Everybody had pretty much what he had, and no one seemed to be paying much attention to anybody else as they conducted diving and flipping contests. He stripped down quickly and jumped in.

"Aw, you shoulda seen it, Nate, it was so funny!" Johnny told him. "We ain't allowed to talk, you know, so we—"

"Not allowed to talk?" Nate interrupted.

"In the breaker? Hell, no! And we wouldn't be able to hear each other anyway. So we have a signal. And when Emil gave it, we all got up together. Bobby ran up the slope and threw a sprag in the works. Mikey whipped a piece of slate at the boss's back—oh boy, was he mad! Then out we went, with him behind us yellin'—"

"—'Come back here, you hoodlums!' " Nate finished the sentence.

"You heard him from here? Hey, fellas! Nate heard the boss from here!" Johnny shouted. The others hooted and howled.

"But what happens now?" Nate asked. "Won't you have to go back?"

"Sure. You'll see, just stick around."

"Then what? Won't he get back at you?"

"Yeah, but"—Johnny shrugged—"who cares? We shut 'em down for a while, and we get to swim." He scrambled out and flipped into the water. "Can you do that?"

"No."

"Come on! Get out, I'll teach you!"

"All right," Nate said uncertainly.

When he climbed out, Johnny pointed at his purple, bruised ribs. "Ooh . . . that what your father did?"

"No. She didn't even tell him."

"She *didn't*? Boy, Nate, she must be nice!"

"I guess."

"So what happened, then?"

"My brother Fr—" He swallowed the name. Did Fred's work ever take him into the breakers? Would the boys know who Fred was? "He did it," Nate finished.

"How come?"

Nate shrugged. "Just for taking up space."

"Takin' up space," Johnny repeated, laughing. "I like that. Anyway, here's what you do. Just step up, like this, with one foot, and throw the whole top part of you forward, and over you go." He demonstrated. Nate's first attempt was a painful belly flop, and he surfaced angry and embarrassed. But Johnny grinned, skimming water into his face. "Try again. You'll get it. Come on."

Nate flipped after five tries—and was surprised by cheers from Mikey, Andre, and Bobby, as well as Johnny. As they circled, each gave Nate a good ducking. He'd always hated that panicky feeling of being held under just a little too long, struggling against a strong hand. But today he had no fear. He knew his friends wouldn't hurt him.

"Nate, Sunday's my birthday," Johnny announced.

"It is? Well, happy birthday!"

"I was wonderin', would you want to come and eat dinner at my house?"

Dinner? Sunday? How would he explain that at home?

"You don't have to, that's awright, I know it's—"

"No, I want to," Nate said. "I *do*. It's just that on Sundays, my father's kind of strict about everybody being home for dinner."

"This would be in the afternoon. We have dinner about three o'clock on Sundays."

"You do?" Nate's family had an early Sunday dinner, too, but not till five. They needn't know where he was going. "Are you sure it's all right? With your parents?"

"I already asked. They said yes."

"All right, I'll be there," Nate said with much more confidence than he felt. He did want to go, but what would it be like, arriving at the patch on his own, spending a whole mealtime with Johnny's family? Would they speak English? Would he be able to eat their food? Would Johnny's parents like him? What about his brothers and sisters?

"Here they come!" someone yelled, and the water bubbled with commotion.

About twenty-five men, mostly miners, marched across the clearing, looking fiercely unhappy. Some carried long whips.

Many of the boys jumped out, scrambling for their clothes. "Stay," Johnny advised, grabbing Nate's arm. "It's better to wait. And when you do get out, watch your *dupa*."

Then the shouting started, back and forth, as the miners joined the breaker boss in cracking braided leather whips at the boys' bare behinds. Nate had no desire to learn what that felt like, so he hid behind Johnny. "What's going on?" he whispered.

"They're our papas. The bosses call them when we go out. They can't work if we don't, see? Coal can't go nowhere if we ain't there."

"Where'd they get those whips?"

"Mule whips. Oh, here comes my papa."

"Yonny!" Johnny's father strode to the water's edge and fired a volley of Polish, which Johnny defiantly returned. Nate dashed into the bushes.

As Johnny hopped into his pants, the breaker boss gave him a resounding crack. He yelped, clapping his hands to his *dupa*.

And then they were running back toward the breaker, boys and men disappearing in a whirlwind of dust and shouts and snapping whips. Left alone with the chirping birds and rippling water, Nate felt relieved—and, at the same time, sorry.

18

NO DOUBT ABOUT IT: a baseball glove was an expensive present for a clerk's son to give. Riding to the patch, Nate was uneasy about bringing it. He'd bought it at Meyer's store, telling Mr. Meyer he'd lost his. Now he had another story ready. But would Johnny believe it?

As Nate approached the house, Johnny stepped into the road, beaming. Nate had never seen him so clean, or so well dressed. He wore black trousers, a plaid shirt, a red waistcoat, and black shoes—and he had a neat, short haircut.

"Wow. What happened to you?" Nate grinned, propping his bike on the porch.

"Mama happened to me! She scrubbed my neck till the skin came off!"

Nate handed him the brown paper sack. "Here."

"You didn't have to bring a present, Nate. I didn't mean you to do that."

"I know. But I wanted to."

"Well, thanks." Johnny opened it, then stared at Nate with his mouth open.

Nate bit his bottom lip. "Is it okay?"

"Is it okay? Is it okay?" Johnny began to laugh. "Nate—how'd you—Nate, you *are* a rich boy, aren't you?"

"No!" he protested, maybe a little too quickly. "Well, my grandfather? He forgets things sometimes, and he just sent me a glove last summer. So I had two, and, well, it's not a catcher's mitt, but"—he shrugged—"I thought you might want to have it."

"Aw, thanks, Nate." Johnny worked his hand into the glove and stroked the leather. "But why don't *you* keep the new one?"

"No chance. I'm just getting the old one the way I want it. I'm not breaking in a new one."

Johnny punched Nate's arm. "*Now* I'd like to see Anton burn my hand! I'm gonna get some neat's-foot oil and oil this glove every night. Damn, I'm gonna *sleep* with this glove every night!" he said, and they laughed. "Come on inside."

Nate hung back. "Wait a minute, I don't know your last name. How can I say hello to your parents?"

"It's Bartelak." Johnny laughed. "Hey, I don't know yours, either!"

"Harper." The name came quickly—not a bad one, either. This deception business was getting easier all the time.

Johnny hauled him inside. "Mama!" He tossed the glove onto his parents' bed. In the kitchen, his mother, cooking with a girl, kept her back to them. "Ma, remember Nate?"

"'Lo, Mrs. Bartelak," Nate mumbled.

She nodded, giving him a bare hint of a smile. Nate's face was on fire; she did not want him here. The tiny room was stifling hot, filled with unfamiliar cooking odors. He couldn't breathe.

"Mama's shy," the girl apologized, eyes gleaming with her smile. "She doesn't speak much English. Hello. I'm Johnny's sister Sofia."

"Hi," Nate said.

Sofia didn't look more than eleven, but she certainly seemed older. And her English was better than Johnny's. That fit with what Nate had heard. The girls went to school while the boys worked in the breakers.

"Everybody outside, Sof?" Johnny asked.

"Yes, except Stefan. He's studying."

"Come on." Johnny pulled Nate away again.

The yard was much nicer. A wooden table was set, with flowers in the middle. Children were running around, and Johnny's father sat with a young man, drinking beer and smoking. They were in waistcoats, shirtsleeves rolled up to their elbows. Mr. Bartelak got up right away, and reached out to Nate with a big smile under his handlebar mustache.

"This is Nate, Papa."

Johnny's father nodded, squeezing Nate's hand in a hard handshake.

"'Lo, Mr. Bartelak."

"Hello. Welcome to our home," Mr. Bartelak said in a thick accent.

"Thank you."

"And this is Machek. I told you—he's our boarder. He's also Papa's butty."

"Chesh," Machek said with a wave.

"Say *chesh*. That means 'hi.'"

"Chesh," Nate said, feeling foolish.

"English, Machek, English," Johnny teased. "You're not in Polska anymore."

Machek's grin showed crooked, broken teeth. Nate wondered about his age—he was more than a boy but less than a man.

"He's only been here a year. He has almost no English. Except 'move'—when *he's* the one taking up the whole bed already," Johnny said accusingly.

Machek understood that perfectly, and chortled as he raised the glass to his lips. He seemed pleasant enough, but Nate couldn't imagine sharing a bed with him.

Johnny's brother Joey was playing a chase game with two small girls. When Johnny caught Joey's arm, they all stopped and gathered around. "Remember Nate?"

"Where's your bike?" was Joey's response.

"Out front. You know how to ride?"

"Yeah," Joey said in a what-do-you-care tone.

Nate shrugged. "You can ride it if you want."

Joey brightened and started off. Johnny grabbed him. "What do you say?"

"Thanks!"

"Be careful!" Johnny called. "And don't let any of your hoodlum friends on it!"

"His friends can ride," Nate said. "I don't mind."

"No," Johnny said simply. He tossed a tiny girl in the air. "This is my little Marta. Aren't you?" She buried her face shyly in Johnny's neck. "She's three. And this is Klara, she's six. Say hello to Nate."

"Hello," Klara said, giggling as she ran off.

The two little girls were blond. Marta's hair was curly, but Klara's was as straight as Johnny's. The girls wore crisp white aprons over dresses with big flowery designs.

"What's over there?" Nate asked, nodding at a high fence made of branches.

"I'll show you." Johnny swung Marta onto his shoulders and opened the rough-hewn gate onto a plot filled with all kinds of flowers and plants.

"Wow!" Nate said. "It's beautiful!" Was there such a garden behind every fence in the patch? If they were visible, the place would look so much nicer. "Why's it hidden away?"

"You have to. Animals would come in. Some people keep a pig, or a cow."

"What're the green ones?" Nate asked, pointing.

Johnny laughed. "The green ones are *vegetables*, Nate." He pointed as they walked: "Squash . . . string beans . . . See the tomatoes? Don't your stepma grow vegetables?"

"Uh, some," he lied.

Marta drummed on Johnny's head. "Yonny, Yonny, *sto lat*," she sang happily.

"Chincooyah," Johnny answered, twisting her bare toes as she giggled. "She said 'Happy birthday,'" he told Nate. "I said 'Thanks.'"

Nate looked at the pretty little face. He could not picture himself lugging Martin or James around that way.

"Yon-ny!" Mrs. Bartelak called.

"Dinner," Johnny said.

Nervously, Nate followed Johnny to the back door, where they washed their hands in a metal basin. He hoped he would be able to sit beside Johnny, but he was too embarrassed to ask.

Breezing past with a platter of food, Sofia playfully pinched Johnny's arm. She and her mother had taken off their cooking aprons to reveal colorfully embroidered blouses. A red ribbon was tied in Sofia's light brown hair. Now Mrs. Bartelak's kerchief was pushed back to reveal hair the same color as Sofia's.

Mrs. Bartelak poked her head inside and shouted impatiently for Stefan, who promptly appeared. "You remember Nate?" Johnny asked him.

"Sure. Hello," Stefan said.

"Hi."

At the table, Mrs. Bartelak spoke to Johnny, pointing out two chairs. "Sit next to me," Johnny said.

Nate was relieved—until Mrs. Bartelak sat right across from him.

"Your bike's okay," Joey announced breathlessly, taking a seat. "I put it on the porch."

"Thanks," Nate said.

"Yozef," Mrs. Bartelak said sharply, and then a few more words.

"Awww," Joey replied. He got up to wash his hands with Klara.

Nate surveyed the platters and bowls. The food was like nothing he had ever seen, except for what seemed to be sausage. What if he took something but couldn't eat it? At home they never had to finish everything. But here, would it be an insult to leave food on his plate?

Johnny's parents began to pass the dishes. At least Nate knew how to do this part. They served themselves at school, too.

"You want some help, Nate?" Johnny asked gently.

Nate sighed with relief, whispering, "Please."

"You like cabbage?"

"It's all right."

"Try this. *Gowompkee.*" He forked one onto Nate's plate. "Mama," Johnny said, followed by a string of Polish. She responded gently. "Mama says try everything, and don't eat anything you don't like."

Nate slowly raised his eyes to hers and heard himself say: *"Chinkayah."*

Everyone burst out laughing, but it didn't make Nate mad. "Very good," Johnny said, thumping his back. "Very close. *Chincooyah.*"

"Chincooyah," Nate repeated.

"You are wel–come," Mrs. Bartelak said, to more laughter.

"Mama!" Johnny exclaimed, clapping his hand to his chest. He turned to Nate: "Mama *never* talks in English!"

Mrs. Bartelak smiled.

"You like sausage?" Johnny asked.

"Yes."

"Kielbasa," Mrs. Bartelak said.

"Kielbasa," Nate repeated.

Johnny gave him a piece. "Now, these you got to try," he said, and served Nate two fat, round dumplings. "Potato and cheese inside." Mrs. Bartelak gestured, giving instructions. "I am, I am," Johnny assured her. He dolloped a spoonful of white stuff onto the dumplings. "Sour cream," he announced, then added a forkful of something golden and stringy: "Fried onions."

Nate looked doubtfully at the conglomeration.

"Pierogi," Johnny told him. "You can't say you had a Polish dinner without *pierogi.* If you don't like it, you don't have to eat it."

Nate was afraid everyone would watch him, but when he looked up they were attending to their own meals. Maybe he should start with what was most familiar. He took a bite of sausage. At home, sausage was only for breakfast. This was spicier, but it was delicious. He ventured on to the *gowompkee,* which was some sort of stuffed cabbage leaves. It was all right, but he might not want to finish it. He took another bite of *kielbasa,* and then a deep breath.

How was Johnny handling this *pierogi* mess? Nate glanced over, then halved the dumpling with his fork, scooping up the toppings. The *pierogi* was sweet and sour and sharp and smooth, all at the same time. When he swallowed, it warmed his stomach. He ate another piece, then another. Mrs. Bartelak nodded approval with a satisfied smile.

"Yonny say you live Hazleton," Mr. Bartelak said.

"Yes."

"You go school, yes?"

"Yes," Nate repeated, pained by the attention. Any more questions and the lies would start to flow. How could he turn the talk away from himself? "How do you say 'yes' in Polish?" he asked Johnny.

"*Tahk,*" Johnny replied.

"And how do you say 'no'?"

"*Nyeh.*" Now Johnny pointed to his mother: "*Matka.*"

"Mother," Nate said.

"*Dobsheh,*" Johnny replied. "Good."

"*Oychets,*" Mr. Bartelak said, indicating himself.

"Father—*tahk?*" Nate said.

"*Tahk,*" Mr. Bartelak agreed.

"*Shostra,*" Johnny said, pointing to his sisters. "*Brat.*" He nodded at Stefan and Joey.

"*Brat?*" Nate repeated. "You're kidding, right?"

"No. Perfect, ain't it?" Johnny asked, and Joey threw a bread ball at him.

Now all were laughing except Machek and Mrs. Bartelak, who tugged on her eldest daughter's arm, obviously puzzled. Sofia explained in Polish; then they joined in the mirth.

Mrs. Bartelak pointed at Nate. "*Shostra?*"

Nate raised three fingers.

"*Brat?*" she asked.

He showed two fingers, but Johnny reached over and pulled up two more. Mrs. Bartelak looked confused. Johnny's explanation included the words *matka* and *oychets* and *brat*. Nodding, Mrs. Bartelak looked sadly at Nate—now he was the pathetic motherless child. He wished he'd raised four fingers to start with. And when he didn't, he wished Johnny had just let it alone.

At that moment, in a sudden rush of noise, about twenty breaker boys filled the yard. They seized Johnny and bore him away on their shoulders.

His family was amused, but where were the boys taking Johnny? Nate didn't know if he should stay or go along. What if the boys told him he was not wanted? But if he didn't go, how long would he be left alone with Johnny's family?

Now the family left the table, too. Nate trailed awkwardly, and Sofia stopped to wait for him. "They're all crazy, those boys," she said happily.

"What are they doing?" Nate asked.

Just then, Mikey dashed back and grabbed Nate's arm, pulling him to catch up with the others, who were singing a boisterous Polish song as they passed Johnny around over their heads. More families came into the street. The boys set Johnny down and lined up with their legs spread. Then Johnny dropped to his hands and knees and scrambled through the tunnel of legs, getting whacked on the *dupa*— hard. But everyone was singing and jeering, and when Nate's turn came he figured he'd better go along with it, and he hit Johnny a wallop.

At the gauntlet's end, Johnny fell in a dramatic heap, holding his *dupa* but still laughing. Now his mother rushed up and yanked him to his feet. Was she angry? She slapped the dust from Johnny's clothes, saying something that caused the boys and spectators to howl. Then she made an announcement, and the boys cheered. Mrs. Bartelak wrapped her arms around Johnny and gave him a big smacking kiss. He shrugged it away, embarrassed, as the crowd started toward the Bartelaks' house.

This was like no birthday party Nate had ever known. Was each one celebrated this way in the patch?

Johnny's eyes searched the group. Nate was proud when Johnny ran to him. "Did you hit me good and hard?"

"As hard as I could," Nate admitted, and Johnny laughed.

In the yard, Mrs. Bartelak, Sofia, and Klara brought plates heaped with doughnuts.

"Ponchkee," Johnny announced, handing him one.

Nate bit into the sweet, warm softness; powdered sugar dissolved on his tongue.

"Mama's are the best in the patch," Johnny said.

Soon Johnny's father was thumping away on an accordion, the adults singing Polish songs, clapping hands, dancing. The little ones shrieked in play, and the older girls grouped together in a circle—just the way Tory and her friends did. Most of the boys drifted back to the street, but Johnny stayed in the yard and Nate kept to his side.

After a while, Nate remembered the time with a jolt. He peeked inside at the kitchen clock: it was nearly five. Grandpa was coming to dinner, and Pa had been very emphatic when he told Nate to be on time. "I have to leave," he said, seizing Johnny's arm.

"Awww."

"No, really. I have to leave *now.*" He looked around. Johnny's father was in the middle of a song. "Tell your father I said thank you. Where's your mother?"

"Okay, okay. Mama!" Nate went with Johnny to his mother, and Johnny said something in Polish.

"Chincooyah," Nate told her, and then said to Johnny, "Tell her dinner was delicious."

Johnny translated; she beamed.

Sofia appeared at her mother's side. "You are leaving?"

"Yes, I have to. I had a wonderful time. Please tell your father."

"I will," Sofia said.

Mrs. Bartelak took Nate's hand and looked at him, saying something in Polish.

"Mama says come and see us again," Sofia translated.

"Tell her I'd like that."

"Say *doeveedzenyah,*" Johnny instructed. "Goodbye."

"Doeveedzenyah."

"Goodbye," Mrs. Bartelak answered.

"Bye," Nate said to Sofia.

"Goodbye, Nate."

Johnny and Nate walked to the front of the house. In the road, the boys were smoking and wrestling. One group was playing some sort of game, flipping cards from a deck. Johnny took Nate's bike off the porch.

"Goin' so soon, Nate?" Andre asked.

"Yeah, I have to leave. My father expects me home."

"Fun ain't even *started* yet," Mikey told him.

Emil just stared suspiciously.

"Wait till I show you fellas what Nate gave me!" Johnny said excitedly.

"Johnny, I have to go." Nate got on his bike. "*Sto lat*. See you tomorrow." He started off, but Johnny ran to catch up, calling his name. Nate stopped.

"Thanks again," Johnny said, shaking his hand. "For the glove and for comin'."

"I really wish I could stay."

Johnny gave him a push and a grin. "Go."

19

WHEN NATE, BREATHLESS, barged through the back door, he found the twins and some younger cousins at the kitchen table. Uncle George's children, Uncle Henry's . . . how much family was at this dinner, anyway? At once Millie and Winnie took up a chant: "Nathan's in trou-ble, Nathan's in trou-ble."

"Shut up," he said.

Mary rushed from the dining room, pleading, "Girls, girls, enough, d' y' not know y' can be heard in there?"

The twins began to giggle; the cousins followed suit.

"Nathan," Mary said to him desperately, "where on earth've y' been, y'—"

Pa stormed in, and without even stopping grabbed the scruff of Nate's neck and pulled him into the front hall. "You simply must challenge me, mustn't you, Nathan?" Pa said, shaking him. "The other night, I made light of your tardiness. Today I specifically requested—no, I *demanded* that you be at the table at precisely five o'clock. And what time is it now?" Pa twisted Nate's face toward the case clock. *"What time is it now?"*

The ship rocked gently on its tin waves. Nate sorely wished he were aboard. "Quarter past," he mumbled, squirming against the pain.

"Quarter past," Pa repeated. "And you're still not ready to present yourself, are you?"

"No, Pa."

Pa released him with a shove. "You've got five minutes."

Upstairs Nate washed quickly, trying to wet his hair into obedience, scowling into the mirror as he plastered it down. Hurriedly he changed into his suit, attempting without success to straighten his tie. Too bad. How did Pa want him— fast or perfect?

Don't think, he told himself on the stairs. *Don't look at anyone.* Silence fell when he entered the dining room. He kept his head down, took his seat, laid his napkin in his lap.

Pa said evenly, "Na-*than.*"

Nate felt his color rise. Fred's snicker was so sneaky, Nate knew he was the only one who could hear it. Slowly he lifted his head. "'Lo, Grandpa. Sorry I'm late."

Grandpa nodded tolerantly.

"'Lo, Uncle George. 'Lo, Aunt Bess." He looked at the adults as he greeted each in turn: Uncle Henry and his wife, Aunt Susan; Aunt Louise, his father's sister, and her husband, Uncle Charles, also a coal operator. Several leaves had been added to the table. There were cousins he hadn't seen in months. He didn't remember when there had been so many to dinner. Why weren't all these people at their summer homes?

Tory gently touched his arm, trying to indicate something.

"Nate?" Pa's question was more like a warning.

Anna! Now his face was frying. She would think he'd slighted her on purpose—and after the other night, that was the last impression he wanted to give. He turned his eyes to her. "'Lo, Anna," he said, then added, "Sorry."

"Hello, Nate," she said with a warm smile.

"I'm glad you could join us, boy!" Grandpa said robustly. "Out exploring the world, eh?"

"Yes, Grandpa."

"Sunny Sunday afternoon, what youngster wants to be in a stuffy house wearing a suit, eh, Nathan?"

"Yes, Grandpa." Nate picked up his spoon, but he was still full from the good Polish food. If he brought the spoon to his mouth a few times, no one but Tory and Mary would notice that he didn't actually eat the soup.

"Nathan's grown a mighty long pair of legs this summer," Pa chuckled. "Wandering who-knows-where on that bicycle of his."

Nate did not even react. What a hypocrite Pa was, with his phony pleasantry.

"Hmm—too busy to stand the old colonel a game of chess?" Grandpa asked.

Nate grinned in response, biting his lip. They hadn't played since last summer. "You think you can still beat me, Grandpa?" he asked, to the adults' amusement.

Across from Nate, his cousin George stared resentfully.

"Well, we'll have to see about that, young fellow," Grandpa said. "I challenge you to a duel tomorrow evening, after dinner."

"I accept," Nate said with a courtly nod.

The ice was broken, but it didn't melt. As the meal progressed, Nate came to realize he wasn't the only one who had brought tension to the table. The adults seemed uneasy. His brothers and older cousins kept exchanging glances. What was going on?

Pa asked Mary to serve the men coffee in the library. As they filed out, Fred with them, it galled Nate that his brother was considered a man. The women took their coffee on the porch; Tory and the girls drifted outdoors, where the younger children were already playing. Nate followed in desperation, unwilling to be left with George.

But George caught up with him and, jerking his head toward the house, asked, "You know what that's all about?"

"No."

"Probably something about the coal."

"Brilliant deduction," Nate said, laughing under his breath.

A few steps later, George tried again. "Where've *you* been lately?"

"Not bothering you and your stupid friends, so what do you care?" Nate retorted.

George sighed, then said with a superior air, "Father says we've got to try to get along, Nate. We'll be working to-gether for the rest of our lives."

"Oh God, what a revolting thought." Nate moaned.

"I don't know why I even bother talking to you," George said contemptuously.

Nate pivoted and walked away. As he started for the hall stairs, Grandpa's voice thundered from the library: "This is still my business, Thomas! Do not presume to tell me how to run my business!"

Nate was chilled. He had never before heard Grandpa shout. And he was shouting at Pa. In front of everybody.

Well, good. Now Pa knew how it felt. Was *he* enjoying it?

In the second-floor hallway, Nate heard singing. "Yessur, yessur, fwee bags full." He touched the nursery doorknob, then hesitated. Hearing Anna's footsteps on the stairs, he sneaked up to the top floor.

Alone in the billiard room, he recalled the afternoon. After he'd gotten over his shyness, he was pretty comfortable at Johnny's house. Too bad Johnny wasn't here right now. It would be fun to show him his soldier box and his climbing tree. Nate would even take Johnny to see the horses.

Nate knew that if his family got to know Johnny, they'd

like him as much as Nate did. But it could never be. Johnny could never meet his family, see his house, eat dinner at his table. *Nate, you are a rich boy, aren't you?* And he'd had to deny it. He had to keep making excuses, both at home and to Johnny.

In the patch, things were so different from what Nate always had imagined. Everybody singing, dancing, eating— happy. And loud! Johnny's father, with his accordion and his friendly face. Johnny's mother . . . Nate recalled Sofia's words: *Mama says come and see us again.*

Johnny probably didn't know how to play billiards, but Nate bet he'd learn fast and shoot well. Nate lined up a shot and hit the ball clean into the corner pocket. "Great shot, Johnny," he said. Then, bowing right and left, he replied, "Thank you. Thank you, one and all."

20

"I'M READY FOR YOU, son!" Grandpa was settled on the porch, with the marble chess pieces all laid out. "Just sitting here plotting my opening strategy."

Nate had never beaten Grandpa at chess, and he wasn't sure he wanted to. It was so important to Grandpa to win. Nate wasn't especially fond of the game; it required far too much thought. But he liked sitting outside on a summer night, drinking lemonade and eating Esther's shortbread cookies, with Grandpa, in carpet slippers, sipping whiskey.

"Heads or tails, Nathan?" Grandpa reached into his pocket.

"Heads."

Grandpa flipped: tails. Nate shrugged. Grandpa tossed him the fifty-cent piece.

"Thanks," Nate mumbled. When he was a child, he liked it when Grandpa gave him the coin. Now it embarrassed him.

Carefully, he turned the board so the white pieces were on Grandpa's side. He tried to focus, but after only a few moves his attention wandered back to the baseball game he'd played that afternoon. The boys had made a big deal over Johnny's new glove, which made Emil seem to dislike Nate even more. Emil played second base, and when Nate slid in for a close play, Emil's tag was more like a punch. Nate had said nothing, hadn't even reacted.

Grandpa handily took Nate's rook with a bishop. "Hah!" he crowed. "Young man, *that* was the sort of move I'd have let you reconsider when you were younger!"

"Hmm. I missed it."

"Before you make a move, you've got to ponder every single possibility. Can he get me? Can *he*? Can *he*?" Grandpa touched the surrounding pawns and knights and bishops and rooks. "Ponder the possibilities," he repeated, just as he had been repeating since Nate was eight years old. "Never get caught out."

"You have to get caught out sometimes, though, don't you, Grandpa?" Nate asked. "Or else there'd be no game."

Grandpa chuckled. "The trick is to know when you're about to be captured," he explained. "Make the move *knowing* what you're about to lose, so as to put yourself in a stronger position."

"Hmm," Nate replied. He tried to follow the advice, but again the game didn't hold his attention. *Sofia thinks you're nice,* Johnny had told him that afternoon, and Nate had blushed fiercely. He didn't give much thought to girls, though Sofia was sweet, and pretty—and smart. But if and when he *did* care about a girl, it certainly couldn't be one from the patch. The notion was even more absurd than being permitted to play with breaker boys.

Grandpa snatched Nate's bishop with a knight. "You play a reckless game, Nathan."

"How'd you *do* that?" Nate asked, staring in puzzlement at the board.

"I set a trap and you walked right into it! Just like the Rebels at Kelly's Ford."

Nate looked up fast. Could it be? A war story he had not heard? "Kelly's Ford?" he asked, pouring a glass of lemonade. "What happened there, Grandpa?"

"It was after the Gettysburg campaign, and we were heading south. One day the boys marched fourteen miles in terrible heat, and they were ready for camp. No sooner was their supper cooking than I was told to give the order to strike tents and pack up quietly, but to leave the fires burning. Oh, I can still hear those boys growling! But I tell you, it was *nothing* compared to what we heard from the Rebel pickets we captured that night! They thought we were in camp, you see. They let down their guard, and we moved in and snapped them up like so many netted herring! *Never* let down your guard, Nathan." He tapped the board. "If you think you know what trick I've got up my sleeve, why, you'd better make sure you look up my other one!" he finished, chortling.

"I'll remember that," Nate said, sitting back to eat a cookie. *Hey, Nate, why don't you come to my house before base-ball?* Johnny had said that afternoon. *You can hang around while I have my bath. Mama won't mind.* Nate liked the idea of spending time at Johnny's. But was it fair to him, this friend-ship based on lies? Eventually one of the boys would find out, or figure out, who he was. Nate knew he must tell Johnny himself. And soon.

But what if the truth turned Johnny against him?

"Pondering the possibilities?" Grandpa asked.

"Yes." Nate had completely forgotten it was his turn. He captured a knight with his king's pawn.

"Check," Grandpa announced with the slide of a rook.

"Ow," Nate said, slumping down.

"Protect your king, young fellow! When he's trapped, his whole army loses! If you continually take the offensive, you'll have to work all that much harder to defend yourself!"

Nate looked up. Was this a serious scold?

Grandpa gave him a wink. "Just as in war," he said, and smiled.

All at once it was quite clear. For Grandpa, playing chess was like reliving the war. Funny that Nate had never seen it before, though he'd been listening to war stories during chess games for four summers. It had been thirty-two years since Appomattox, and Grandpa was still fighting.

Nate scrambled to reverse the damage, but it was no use.

"Checkmate," the old colonel said.

21

AT HOME they'd have been shocked by bathtime at Johnny's. Stefan and Machek and Johnny stripped down without a trace of shame, right in front of Mrs. Bartelak, and at the metal tub she scrubbed each black neck. There was plenty of joking and teasing, all in Polish. When Johnny translated, Nate's face burned.

Johnny's father was never around in the afternoon. He and the other miners always went to the tavern after work. A beer and a whiskey helped clear the coal dust from their lungs, Johnny said.

At first Nate had made it a point not to watch the baths. But everybody noticed, and then they teased *him*. So he quickly learned to act as they did, as if it were no big deal. He sat nearby, eating whatever Mrs. Bartelak offered—fruit, a cookie, fried dough with sugar—until Johnny was ready.

Mrs. Bartelak always seemed cheerful now. Except the day it rained.

The drizzle began when Nate met Johnny at the top of the patch. By the time they reached the house, it was pelting down in sheets. From the road, they heard Johnny's mother yelling.

When they entered the house, Mrs. Bartelak and Sofia were running up the stairs. Johnny followed them, and Nate followed Johnny. Stefan stood on a chair, holding the ceiling up, it seemed. When he saw Johnny, he rattled off something in Polish. Johnny took his place, and Stefan dashed out. Mrs. Bartelak and Sofia tried to catch the rain in buckets, but everything was soaked. Water ran down Johnny's arms and splashed his face. The younger children crowded in the doorway as Mrs. Bartelak shouted and shook her fists.

Nate didn't need to guess whom she was cursing. Again and again, he heard his own last name.

Hammers and rain pounded the roof. Over the racket, Johnny shouted back and forth to Stefan and Machek. Finally the rain let up, the roof seemed to be mended, and Mrs. Bartelak, still ranting, snatched up the wet bedclothes and marched downstairs with the girls.

Johnny stepped down and sighed. "Every time it rains."

"Every time?" Nate echoed.

"Yep."

"Can't you get them to fix it?" Nate's voice was as parched as his throat.

"Nope."

If it happened every time, why hadn't Johnny's father come to help? Surely he knew it was raining. And surely he knew water poured into their house.

"It's no big deal, Nate. Just a little water," Johnny said as if reading his mind.

"Your mother seemed to think it was a big deal."

Johnny shrugged, grinning. "Papa says she likes it because it gives her another reason to curse the company." He reached under the bed for his glove. "It's clearin' up already. Let's go."

Another afternoon, Sofia wasn't there when Nate and Johnny arrived. But a few minutes later, she parked a wagon full of coal bits by the kitchen door. Nate went to help.

"Oh, don't," she said, turning up blackened palms. "You'll get filthy."

"Do I look like I'd care?" he replied, and she laughed.

They brought the wagon inside and emptied its contents into the bin by the stove.

When the job was finished, Nate stammered, "Um—Sofia?"

She turned to him.

"The culm banks, I—I hear they can slide. It's dangerous, what you do."

"Yes," she said.

"Then why do you do it?"

"Mama says, 'Sofia, we need coal.'" She wiped her hands on her apron, looked up at him, and smiled. "That means I must go."

22

SWINGING PA'S LEATHER STRAP, Nate stalked the library, practicing the poem he'd chosen, about a servant who carried water to wounded soldiers in India:

> *"It was 'Din! Din! Din!*
> *''Ere's a beggar with a bullet through 'is spleen;*
> *''E's chawin' up the ground,*
> *'An' 'e's kickin' all around:*
> *'For Gawd's sake git the water, Gunga Din!'"*

"Very good, Nate." Mr. Hawthorne smiled, looking up from checking Nate's arithmetic. "You might have a future in the theater."

"Nah." Nate threw himself into Pa's armchair. "I have a future in a colliery."

Mr. Hawthorne peered over the top of his glasses. "Only if you want it, surely."

"All the boys go into the family business," Nate said wearily. "That's how it works. My grandfather says I'll start in coal, just like everyone else." To change the subject, he nodded at his arithmetic paper, which lay on the desk in front of Mr. Hawthorne. "How'd I do?"

"You did tolerably well. I'll be making up a set of lessons for you to take to Cape May next week, and I—"

"Cape May!" Nate groaned, burying his face in his hands. He'd been so busy with Johnny and with lessons, he had forgotten all about it. Or maybe he'd willed himself to forget.

"Do I sense that you are not looking forward to this expedition?" Mr. Hawthorne said wryly.

"I forgot," Nate admitted. "And there's other things I'd rather do."

"Such as?"

"Such as sitting here memorizing the names of the Seven Hills of Rome."

"No need for sarcasm, sir."

Nate paced, his hands behind his back. If he went to the shore, he'd lose his spot at third base, he'd miss the game against the Lattimer breaker—but, even worse, how would he explain his absence to Johnny?

"Nathan?" Mr. Hawthorne said. "Are you listening to me?"

"Huh?"

"I said, for your impertinence you may recite them now."

"Mons Quirinalis," Nate droned. "Mons Viminalis. Mons Av . . . Av . . ."

"Aventinus."

"Yeah, that. Mons Caelius. Mons Cap . . . Cap . . ."

"Capitolinus. Continue."

"Mons . . . Oh, I don't know!" Nate dropped into the chair again, then slithered to the floor in a heap.

"Esquilinus," Mr. Hawthorne reminded him, starting to pack up. "Go on."

"No!"

"Mons Palatinus. On your feet, please, young man."

Nate stood.

"I expect your full cooperation tomorrow. You've been doing so well, and I *would* like to give your father a good report."

"All right," Nate agreed, seeing him to the door.

"I'll leave you with a bit of advice that will serve you well throughout life." Mr. Hawthorne sounded unlike himself, very serious and stern. "Would you like to hear it?"

"Go ahead."

"*Semper ubi sub ubi,*" Mr. Hawthorne said solemnly. He headed down the stairs, swinging his valise in a carefree manner.

Semper ubi sub ubi. Nate called out doubtfully, "Always wear underwear"?

Mr. Hawthorne's backward wave acknowledged the translation. Laughing, Nate went inside.

Pa liked to stand on the porch after lunch, smoking a pipe and looking around the grounds. Today Nate followed him outside and asked, "Pa?"

"Yes, Nathan!" Pa said heartily.

"I was thinking that maybe I wouldn't have to go to the shore this year."

Pa frowned, shaking out his match. "Why ever not? You love the shore."

"I don't know. I'd rather stay here."

"Nonsense, Nate!"

Anna came out, holding Martin's hand and followed by Lucy, who carried James. "What's nonsense?" Anna asked brightly.

Nate gritted his teeth. Did she never mind her own business? A few words alone with his father, was that too much to ask?

"He doesn't want to go to the shore," Pa grumbled, making a dismissive gesture at Nate. Then he turned to Anna's boys. "Are you going to dreamland, Jamesy?"

There was that dopey voice. Nate had to roll his eyes—and Anna, of course, had to see.

Pa kissed James with a loud smack. "Papa will see you after work. All right, my little man? And my Marty . . ." He swung the boy into his arms.

Nate gripped the porch rail, staring across the lawn. Pa had never held him that way, he was sure of it. And he couldn't recall Pa ever kissing him. Not once.

Anna stood beside him as Pa continued talking gibberish. "Not go to the shore?" she said.

"I was speaking to *Pa* about it," Nate said pointedly.

Anna looked startled. "All right, Lucy, it's time," she said, whisking the three back inside.

"Couldn't I just stay here with Mary?" Nate asked Pa.

"The staff take their vacation when we do, Nathan," Pa said. "With the exception of Patrick, and I don't envision him caring for you."

"I don't need care!" Nate protested. "And I could take meals with Grandpa."

"Nathan!" Pa said sharply. "Enough! I don't know what's

gotten into you, but I've had plenty of it! You'll go to the shore, and we'll hear no more on the topic!"

Patrick brought the landau up. "Tom! Fred!" Pa called. "Good afternoon, dear," he said, kissing Anna. Nate averted his eyes.

"And to you, darling," Anna replied.

As Nate's brothers passed, Tom tousled his hair and Fred pinched his arm hard. Pa descended the stairs behind them and climbed into the carriage. Nate turned to the house.

"Nathan," Anna said. He stopped. "I think you've come to the age," she began deliberately, "at which a boy prefers to be with his friends rather than his family. Shall I try to explain that to your father? Perhaps he'll relent and allow you to stay."

Nate was about to give an enthusiastic "Yes!" when he realized Anna had set him a trap—and he'd been ready to walk right into it, just like the Rebel pickets at Kelly's Ford. If he said yes, he was admitting he had friends. If he admitted he had friends, she would ask who they were.

"No, thank you," he said steadily. "I think I've come to the age at which I ought to stand up for myself." He faked a smile. "Don't you agree?"

She didn't smile back. "Nate. Where do you go every afternoon?"

He set his jaw. "I ride my bike."

"Where to?"

"Here and there."

"I was in Meyer's store the other day, looking at wallpaper. Mr. Meyer said you'd bought a baseball glove."

"I lost mine." Nate stared hard at her. "I didn't want Pa to know, so I bought another."

Anna nodded. "I see."

He started down the stairs.

"Your pa's given you a great deal of freedom this summer," she called. He froze. "If you were doing something he wouldn't approve of, he might think it prudent to keep you on the grounds. More closely supervised."

"Thank you," Nate said. "I'll remember that."

Then he continued walking.

23

ALL WEEK AT BASEBALL, Nate acted as though there were nothing wrong. He was certain that Pa wouldn't change his mind, but kept the hope that somehow he'd be able to stay home. Each time Saturday swam to the surface of his mind, he pushed it under again.

"Have you begun to pack yet, Nate?" Anna would gently ask.

"Not yet" was his pleasant reply, time after time.

The breaker boys were excited about the Lattimer game, planned for Saturday. Nate knew he should give notice if he couldn't play, because someone else would need practice at third base.

Thursday at breakfast, he decided to try again. "Pa?"

"Yes, Nate?" Pa said, buttering his toast.

"I was wondering if you'd think it over. About my staying home."

With forced patience, Pa put his knife down, blinked a few times, looked at Nate. "Nathan, I made it quite clear—"

"But don't you think it's best if I continue my lessons with Mr. Hawthorne?"

Tom and Fred broke into disbelieving laughter.

"Oh, so that's your motivation, is it?" Pa chuckled, looking from Tom to Fred. "Scholastic excellence?"

His brothers found this even funnier. Nate burned with anger and humiliation.

"Stop it, you two!" Tory cried, jumping up. "You're both horrid!"

"Tory . . ." Pa said soothingly, but she rushed from the room. "Look, Nathan, I want to hear no more about this, do you understand?" Pa wagged a warning finger. "I want your bags packed and a smile on your face. Is that clear?"

"Yes," Nate said. "May I be excused?"

"No!" Pa snapped. "Eat your breakfast!"

That afternoon, Nate finally told Johnny. "I might not be able to play Lattimer."

Johnny frowned. "Why?"

"Well, my grandfather's sick. I have to go to Philadelphia to see him."

"Aw, Nate, can't you go after Saturday? We'll need you to beat the Dagos—Anton says you're our best third baseman by far!"

Nate couldn't enjoy the compliment because he had to concentrate on the lie. "Well, the thing is, he's very sick. His heart. They think he might die."

"*Really?*" Johnny's dismay made Nate sick from his own treachery, and when Johnny patted his shoulder he felt even worse. "That's rotten, Nate. I'm sorry. Well, you gotta go then, sure. You better tell Anton, though."

"Will you tell him for me?"

Johnny grinned. "You ain't scared of Anton, are you?"

"Maybe a little," Nate admitted.

Johnny punched his arm and trotted over to Anton. As Johnny talked, he gestured toward Nate. Emil joined them. Anton didn't say much, and Emil kept glaring at Nate. Finally Anton called out, "Okay, Nate to right field. Luka to short. Bobby, third base!"

24

"WHILE YOU'RE AWAY," Mr. Hawthorne said after Friday's session, "I'd like you to learn the conjugations of two new verbs: present, imperfect, future, and present subjunctive."

"Okay." Nate ran his finger along a row of smooth leather bookbindings.

"I haven't heard you practice 'Gunga Din' lately, Nathan," Mr. Hawthorne said affably.

Nate shrugged. "I'm not in the mood."

"Yes, you've been awfully gloomy for a boy who's going to the shore."

Nate didn't respond. They walked to the front hall.

"At any rate," Mr. Hawthorne continued, "memorize the next stanza. And I've worked up some arithmetic problems. And read along in *The Deerslayer*. But do enjoy yourself, Nate."

Pa entered with Tom and Fred, who greeted Mr. Hawthorne and continued to the dining room. "Mr. Hawthorne," Pa said, shaking his hand. "How are the studies going?"

"Very well, Mr. Tanner. Nate's making excellent progress. I've given him his marching orders, but he needn't work terribly hard."

"Good news, Nate," Pa said. "And about time, too. Run along to lunch; I'd like a private word with Mr. Hawthorne."

Nate scuffled away. Why was it impossible for Pa to give him a compliment without taking it back in the next breath? Sliding into his chair, Nate prodded the white soup with his spoon. "What in heck is this?"

"Nathan," Anna said with quiet disapproval.

"It's cucumber soup," Mary said indignantly. "I thought I'd try something new."

Nate filled his spoon, then dumped the contents back.

"Nathan!" Anna repeated, just as Pa walked in and Mary flounced out.

"Problem?" Pa asked, kissing Anna's cheek.

"No, dear," Anna said with a smile.

"Nate's making fun of the soup," one of the twins blurted out, and Nate glared at her.

Pa bowed his head for a moment of thanks. They all did the same.

Nate took a tentative taste of the thick white stuff. "It's cold!" he protested, coughing dramatically, rubbing the back of his hand across his lips.

"Use your napkin, dear," Anna said, while Tom and Fred snickered.

"You've eaten chilled soup before," Pa said patiently.

"None made of cucumbers." Nate submerged his spoon again. This time he lifted it higher to let the soup spill into the bowl. It splattered Tory's arm. "Sorry, Tor." He dabbed her arm with his napkin. She just sat, tight-lipped.

"I think it's delicious," Anna said lightly as Mary returned with a platter of chicken salad. "Give it a chance, Nate."

He laid his spoon down and, looking at Mary, said, "I'd rather *not*."

Mary squinted at him.

"You're missing a treat, Nathan," Pa said cheerfully. "Mary, the soup is lovely."

"Thank *you*, Mr. Tanner," Mary replied.

When she stood at Nate's left with the salad, he mumbled, "Please," and she filled his plate.

"I, for one, am quite looking forward to being on that train tomorrow," Pa said. "Anna, I can't wait to see what the boys make of the ocean this year."

The boys. Always the boys. As if he had no other sons. As if nobody else existed.

"Now, Tom," Pa went on, "while we're gone I'd like you to be sure to—"

"What!" Nate dropped his fork with a clatter. The exclamation escaped before he could shut his mouth on it, and now that mouth just kept moving. "What do you mean, while *we're* gone? Isn't he coming?"

"I've been invited to spend two weeks in the mountains with Alice's family," Tom explained. "At the end of the month. So I'll continue at the collieries until then."

"Well, if *he'll* be here, why can't I stay with him?" Nate asked, turning to Pa.

Pa fixed him with a dazed stare. "Because *I* say you're going to the shore," he said evenly. "And I have told you *twice* already that I do not wish to be questioned further on the matter!"

"Change is difficult at times," Anna said. "I'm sure once you get there, you'll—"

"Hate it!" Nate said. "I *don't* want to go!"

Pa slapped the table. "That is enough! You think your life is so terrible, Nathan? Here in the lap of luxury? All right, then it's time you saw boys who have no such worries as spending two weeks at the shore! You'll tour the breaker with me this afternoon and see how you'd like to *be* one of those boys!"

Nate sat back, the room oozing and whirling. He'd gone too far. The breaker. This afternoon. Was there any way out?

"Pa," he began apologetically. "I only—"

"I said, enough!" Pa was purple with rage. "Finish your lunch in the kitchen! And don't dare to leave this house! You'll be ready when Patrick comes or I'll thrash you within an inch of your life!"

Nate's legs felt rubbery as he slowly stood, picked up his plate, walked through the pantry.

"I tell you, Anna, just when I hear a good word about him . . ." he heard Pa complain.

"Y' always push him, Nathan," Mary said. "Always."

He clapped his plate onto the kitchen table and dropped into a chair.

The four breakers on the south side were the closest. But maybe Pa would take him to Brookdale or High Ridge or Banbury instead of Harland. Nate had a seventy-five percent chance of being spared. Excellent odds, for most people. But with his luck . . .

"Well, now y'll have a look at a different life, eh?" Mary told him. "Y'll see what Pat did when he was a boy."

"Patrick worked in the breaker?" Nate asked, to take his mind off his misery.

"Y' knew that, surely."

"No I didn't . . . I guess I did . . . Oh, *I* don't know."

"If y' ever listened, y' might hear something every so often." Mary sat across from him. "Pat worked in the breaker till he was fourteen, and then he went below. Tended door for two years."

"A nipper?"

"That's right, and then he was his da's butty." The next part Nate knew. "Their chamber caved in. Pat's da was killed, and Pat and some others were trapped for three days before the rescuers got to them. Pat's ma was beside herself, between the worry and the grief. And y'r da went to visit her every day." She tapped the table. Nate looked up; this he had not heard before. "Paid for all the funeral expenses, he did."

"Well, he ought to've," Nate grumbled. "It's his mine that killed her husband."

"You listen here, Nathan," Mary said sternly. "The miners know what kind of work they're takin' on. They go down to make a better life than the one they come from, in Ireland, or Poland, or Italy, or what-have-y'. And when there's an accident—well, that's part of the job. After Pat's da was killed, y'r da brought Pat to work in this house out of respect for Pat's ma. And Pat's ma said to her dying day that she was grateful to y'r da for gettin' Pat out of the mines."

Nate pushed salad around his plate. Mary stood to spoon dessert into crystal cups.

"After that cave-in was when y'r grandfather decided, no more fathers havin' sons as butties. They've got to work far apart now, to lessen the chance of two in the same family bein' killed at once."

So that was the reason for the rule. *They're just mean,* Johnny had said—and Nate had been quite willing to believe it. Was Johnny wrong about other things?

Mary placed a cup of raspberry sherbet before him. He pushed it away and laid his head on the table. "Y're actin' awfully peculiar," she said. "Are y' feelin' ill?"

"No. I mean yes. Would you tell Pa I'm not well and I can't go?"

Mary gave her lilting laugh and walked out with the tray. When she returned, she said, "Get y'r head off the table, Nathan. It's unsanit'ry."

"I can't go to the breaker," he moaned, closing his eyes.

"And why not? Too good for it, are y'?"

Nate took a deep breath: it was time. "Mary? Can I tell you something?"

The screen door creaked. Harry and Patrick were coming in for their lunch. Nate's eyes met Patrick's, then both looked quickly away.

"Hallo, Nate!" Harry said.

"'Lo, Harry." Nate scraped his chair back. He bet they didn't have to eat cucumber soup.

"Remember what y'r da said," Mary called as he headed for the door.

"I'll be on the porch," Nate replied. In the front hall he retrieved his plaid cap, which he hated and never wore.

Later, when Patrick brought the carriage around, he asked, "Sir?"

"Fred and Tom to High Ridge, Patrick," Pa replied.

Nate shut his eyes and bit his lip.

Pa said, "And then go to Harland."

25

"HOLD THE RAILING, Nathan!" Pa shouted over his shoulder as they climbed the breaker stairs. If he bothered to turn around, he'd know his breath had been wasted. Nate was already gripping both sides tight.

The coal cars' clamor and clashing, loud even when heard

from the ground, was much worse up here. Inside, the noise was deafening, and Nate could barely see in front of him.

At first he thought it was the normal switch from bright sun to indoors. But as he and Pa kept climbing, his eyes didn't adjust. The breaker had hundreds of tiny window-panes. So where was the light?

Turning to the windows, he understood: coal dust. It blackened the glass, clouded the air, closed his throat. His body protested with a coughing fit.

And then he saw the breaker boys.

They sat two by two on wooden benches, straddling chutes down which coal crashed in a steady tumult. Heads bent, hands in the chutes, fingers moving swiftly, they picked out the slate and flicked it into a separate chute.

Nate's hopes soared—maybe they wouldn't see him at all, standing behind them as he was—but then Pa took his arm and continued up the steps. Nate hung back, his dread about to strangle him. With an angry frown, Pa tugged him onward.

Fool, Nate told himself. Why hadn't he run when he had the chance? Yet even in his despair, he was curious. Which one was Johnny? They all looked the same, hunched over their work, caps low on their foreheads, scarves over their mouths. Nate yanked the ugly plaid cap nearly over his eyes. Maybe they wouldn't recognize him, either, through the hazy dust, in the dim light.

The breaker boss held a long stick. He poked it into the coal chute, then into someone's back.

The boy jumped and so did Nate, heart pounding even harder. "Pa!" he protested.

Pa didn't hear.

Surely the boy would do something, say something. But he just hunkered down and continued picking slate.

Now the boss saw Pa, and a big smile spread over his face. As he walked to them, the boys craned their necks to see who merited such a welcome. Nate stepped behind Pa, but Pa pulled him forward, shouting, "This is my middle boy, Nathan!"

The breaker boys could not have heard the introduction, because Nate barely heard it himself. But two eyes caught his—Emil's. Nate knew he could not, would not, hide any longer.

A new load of coal roared into the breaker. Huge toothed rollers chewed it up and spat it down the chute. The boys worked their legs, pushing coal behind them with their heels as they picked out the slate.

All except Emil. He pulled his scarf from his mouth, turned his head slightly, and spat tobacco juice, never taking his eyes off Nate's. Then he elbowed the boy beside him.

Pa and the boss talked with their heads together as each boy signaled and poked those nearby. One by one by one they turned, one by one by one they pulled the scarves from their mouths. Nate saw Bobby and Mikey, Andre and Luka, all the others who played baseball. And then he saw Johnny.

Johnny stood slowly, his jaw dropping open, moving toward Nate as if sleepwalking. Nate was terrified—not for himself, but for Johnny. The others seemed to share his fear. As Johnny walked past them, each boy tugged at his arms, trying to stop him, to pull him down.

But Johnny shook them off and finally halted, glaring at Nate, his face filled with confusion and betrayal. When Nate could bear it no longer, he turned his back and tried to concentrate on hearing Pa and the boss. The boss gestured, and Nate trailed Pa up the steps. The man at the top tipped another car's contents into the machinery. Heads down, backs bent, the boys were at work again. Or so it seemed.

Something hit Nate, hard, between the shoulder blades; he flinched from the pain. Pa didn't notice—but the boss did, and somehow he knew who was guilty. Brandishing his stick, he stomped down the steps. As Johnny cowered, protecting his head, the boss whacked him once, twice, three times across the shoulders.

"What happened, Nate?" Pa shouted near his ear.

Nate was sick with anger and fear, but he said nothing.

The boss strode back, making apologetic gestures, patting Nate's back. He wore an ingratiating smile.

"Get your stinking hands off me," Nate muttered, feeling his voice shake.

But neither the boss nor Pa nor Nate himself heard the words.

At the breaker's summit, Pa turned Nate around to watch the boys. How could it be? How could they work all day, five days a week, sometimes six, in this dusty, noisy, smelly place, heads bowed, eyes down, this wretched man hanging over them with his stick? These were not the boys who laughed and fought and played and cursed. These were not the boys he knew.

As Nate watched, he realized that their fast-moving fingers were doing more than picking slate. *We have a signal,* Johnny had said. Of course, this was how the boys talked while they worked—and there could be no doubt of what they were talking about now.

But Johnny paid no attention. His head was practically in the chute; furiously, he kicked coal behind him and flung bits of slate.

Nate turned away, and didn't look again.

"Well, Nate," Pa said in the colliery yard. "What do you think? Are you ready to go to the shore now?"

"Yes, Pa." Downcast, defeated, he wanted only to be dismissed, to be in his room alone.

"Patrick!" Pa called. "Take Nathan home, please."

"Sir," Patrick said.

Nate climbed in.

"Remember this day," Pa said with his superior air, "whenever you decide to feel sorry for yourself."

Oh, he'd remember it, all right. This was one day he would never forget.

Patrick clucked to the horses.

Nate wrapped himself tight in his shame, staring at nothing as Patrick drove home.

"Nathan?" Mary turned from her work as he slammed in through the kitchen and started up the back stairs. "Nate?" she called in the stairwell.

He ran on, past the entrance to the servants' quarters, past the second-floor landing. But when he reached his room, nearly safe at last, there was Fiona, rummaging in the wardrobe—and his soldier box was on the floor.

"What are you doing?" he asked.

Startled, Fiona dropped an armful of clothing.

"What are you doing?" he repeated, louder.

"I'm packin' your bags, Nathan."

"Who said you could come in my room and go through my things?"

"I'm not goin' through anything!" she said indignantly. "I was packin' your bags like your mother asked me to."

The white-hot light flashed in Nate's eyes. "She—is—not—my—mother!" His fury gave a separate breath to each word. "And she has *no* right sending servants into my room to go through my things! Get out!"

When Fiona scuttled past, he slammed the door, then grabbed the soldier box. Dizzy with panic, he opened it and counted the soldiers. Then he backed up to the wall, sliding down by inches until he was on the floor, knees drawn to his chest. Why did he ever think he'd be able to have a friend? He was a liar, a fake, and a fool. He had no friends—never did, never would.

Nate put his head down on the soldier box. "Never," he said.

The lone word echoed in the large, silent room.

Later he crept down the back steps, on the lookout to avoid Fiona and Anna. If he made it through the kitchen, he wouldn't have to speak to anyone. He'd go to the farthest corner of the grounds, up into the copper beech. There, hidden in the leaves, he could forget the whole world and everybody in it.

But Fiona's voice stopped him cold.

"Say what you will, Mary, he's nothin' but a pack of trouble."

"Ah, I don't know, Fee. He can be sweet when he wants to be."

"Hmpph! Trouble is, he *never* wants to be!"

When Mary snickered in reply, Nate leaned all his weight on the wall, feeling as if he'd been punched in the gut.

"Still," Mary said, "I've a soft spot for him, Fee. He isn't the same since she's gone. I wish y'd known him then. How she doted on him!" Mary sighed deeply.

Nate shut his eyes tight.

"Hard to imagine," Fiona said. "He's so nasty, most of the time."

"I know, 'tisn't easy to like him sometimes," Mary admitted. "But I feel I'm keepin' care of him . . . for her. *That's* how I think of it."

"Well, that's good of you, Mary." A chair grated against the floor. Fiona said, "Thanks for a nice cuppa, and the chat. I must go up and—"

Nate didn't hear the rest. He turned and headed back to his room, and shut himself in till dinnertime.

26

HIS EXCUSE WAS his schoolwork.

Come to the beach, Pa said. *Let's go for a walk,* Tory suggested. *Why aren't you in the water, dear?* Anna asked.

I have to learn Latin verbs. Memorize "Gunga Din." Do arithmetic.

"But, Nate," protested Pa, who had been acting so kind since dragging him into the breaker, "Mr. Hawthorne said you needn't work too hard."

"I *want* to work hard," Nate answered with phony sincerity. "I don't want to fall behind when the term begins."

Pa gave a disgruntled shake of his head and walked off the hotel porch, where Nate spent most days so he wouldn't have to see the blue sky or bright sun, the white sand or glittering ocean.

Tory brought him saltwater taffy from shopping trips with the twins; this he didn't refuse. "We made *such* a grand sandcastle," she said one afternoon. "The moat is so big, Martin and James are sitting in it! Won't you come see?"

"I have to conjugate."

"You do not!" she retorted, and he looked up in surprise. "Pa says you're being difficult. And he says we're all to ignore you."

"Then I've no doubt you'll obey him," Nate shot back.

"You wouldn't dare tarnish your image as the world's most perfect daughter."

Her eyes flashed with hurt, and her mouth quivered. At once he regretted the words—but he just held *The Deerslayer* in front of his face.

"Honestly, Nathan," she said, turning away. "You're getting worse and worse."

Nate snapped the book shut and bit his lip, scowling as he watched her go.

But he felt he *had* to make himself miserable, after all he'd seen in the breaker—and after being seen there. How could he let himself enjoy things, knowing how Johnny and the others spent their workdays, imagining what Johnny must think of him now? Well, he probably would never see Johnny again, so it hardly mattered.

Worse and worse. Tory was right. He hadn't felt this bad since Mama died. But the death of friendship was death of a different kind—the death of hope. Nothing would change for him; he would always be unhappy. And nasty, just as Fiona had said.

Of course it was all too clear now. He should have told Johnny who he was from the start, instead of stacking lies atop lies like the blocks on Martin's tower, destined to come crashing down. And yet, if Pa hadn't taken him to the breaker, he'd still be working on his castle of deception.

"Nate, boy!" Fred tromped onto the porch, where Nate lay on his stomach. "What makes you so studious these days?" With a motion so swift Nate couldn't head it off, Fred swooped down and snatched the poetry book. "'Gunga Din'!" Fred hooted.

"Give it back." Nate jumped up, reaching.

"Not so fast. 'Gunga Din,' eh? I remember 'Gunga Din.' Let me hear you recite it."

"I don't know it yet," Nate lied, and then lied twice more: "My tutor chose it, and I hate it."

"It *is* the stupidest poem ever written, I'll grant you that. What imbecile would get his own head blown off just to bring water to some fellow who's been beating him for months? I don't imagine you'd bring *me* water under fire, would you?"

Nate lunged again, but Fred clutched the book to his chest and settled into a bright-blue rocker.

"So, Nate, boy. What's all the moping for? It's because of your little visit to the breaker, isn't it?"

Nate shot him a suspicious look.

"Ah, I've hit it, haven't I?" Fred said with a smirk. Then he spoke in a high, simpering voice: "Oh, the poor little Hunkies in the breaker, they have such hard lives, isn't it *awful*?" He shook his head. "I thought so, too, first time I went in. But I got over it fast. And so will you, when you see what goes on down below."

Nate thought of Johnny saying *I can't wait till I get down below*. Grudgingly, he asked his brother, "What's *that* supposed to mean?"

Fred snorted in disgust, shaking his head. "Those miners do whatever they damn well please. Defying the boss right to his face. Then off they go to the tavern to get drunk every afternoon. And the mule boys, taking their sweet time in the gangway, like *they* own the place." He fanned the book's pages with his thumb. "Oh, and then there's the spraggers. They've been told a hundred times not to ride on the cars. But when they smash their stupid heads on the rocks, they blame the company. So don't feel too sorry for the breaker boys, chump. They're just biding their time till they can go below and raise hell."

"Well, what kind of life is that?" Nate mumbled.

"No kind for me." Fred tossed him the book. "I tell you, *I've* seen enough of it. I'm getting away from the stinking coal as fast as I can. Makes a fellow glad his great-grandfather was the last poor person in the family, huh? And knew what to do when he found the coal."

"Makes *this* fellow wish his great-grandfather never did," Nate said.

"Oh, you *do* have it bad! The poor-old-miner blues. Maybe you should join the workers' union!" Heartily enjoying his own humor, Fred headed inside. "You'll change your tune," he called. "Just wait and see."

Nate clutched the porch rail, staring at the ocean. *I got over it fast. And so will you.* But he would never be like Fred. Or would he? When Pa was young, what did he think about the boys working the mines? Nate squeezed his eyes shut and forced his thoughts to Latin. *Conjugate two new verbs.* He rested his head on the porch post and said: *"Odi, odisti, odit."*

I hate, you hate, he hates.

27

THEY RETURNED from Cape May on a Sunday night, the twenty-second of August. The next day, Nate had his lessons with Mr. Hawthorne, then moped around the grounds all afternoon. But when he heard the breaker whistle, he knew what he must do.

Now Johnny's going down the stairs, he thought as he did the same. *Now he's walking past the culm banks.* Nate got his bike but left his glove. Riding through the service gate, he pictured Johnny clowning on the patch road with the others.

Now the boys are disappearing into their yards. Now Johnny's having his turn at the tub, drying himself with the rough towel, getting into clean clothes. Nate rode steadily toward the baseball field. Would Johnny even look at him? What would Emil say, or Anton? What if they jeered and threw rocks at him?

It didn't matter. He had to go and show his face. Despite his fear. Despite his shame.

No . . . *because* of it.

Cheers and chatter floated up from the field as Nate approached. But when he stopped at the top of the rise, the boys fell silent.

Behind home plate, Johnny straightened up. They locked eyes. Slowly Johnny crossed over to him. The racket in Nate's ears was as loud as coal tumbling down the breaker chute.

Johnny looked mean and hateful—ready to spit or hit, Nate thought. Instead, Johnny grabbed Nate's wrist, yanking his arm forward. Nate flinched, and despised himself for it. Then Johnny slapped his baseball glove into Nate's hand and turned away.

Nate let the glove fall. "Johnny."

Johnny kept walking.

"I wanted to tell you," Nate said.

Johnny wheeled around, rushed back to Nate, and shoved the heel of his hand into Nate's chest, causing him to stumble. "Oh yeah? You did?" Johnny pushed him again. "Then why in hell didn't you? Huh?"

Now Johnny pushed Nate with both hands, but Nate didn't even want to fight back. He just bit his lip to keep from crying.

"You made a fool of me in there," Johnny spat out. "In front of them." He jerked his head toward the others. "But worse—you *lied* to me. Clerk. Harper. Just moved here, grandfather in Philadelphia." The fourth push was close to a punch. "Grandfather in a castle on top of Hazleton, and you in another, lookin' down at all the Hunkies who work for you."

Nate stared at the ground and shook his head. "I don't," he managed to say, pushing his hands into his pockets.

"Just go home, *Tanner*," Johnny said, kicking dirt at him. "Go home."

Nate started down the rise. Johnny hurled the glove in an arc so it landed in Nate's path.

"And take your glove!"

"It's *your* glove," Nate called. "I gave it to you."

"Well, I don't want your damn handouts!"

At that, anger defeated sorrow, and Nate stalked back. "It was no handout, and you know it," he said fiercely. "It was a present. Because I thought you were my friend."

"Oh, yeah?" Johnny shouted. "What about what *I* thought? Huh? You lied to me! You lied about everything! What kind of friend is that? And what did you lie for? Tell me that, huh? What for?"

Nate let out his breath and frowned, looking into the distance. "Because I wanted to play." He shrugged. "That's all. I liked you. And I wanted to play." He kicked the glove hard and headed for his bike.

There was a running yell and Johnny landed on Nate's back, punching his head until Nate flipped him over his shoulders. Johnny dragged Nate to the ground, and as they pounded each other, the breaker boys poured noisily over the rise. Nate got in a good gut punch, but then Johnny grabbed Nate's face, twisting his neck. Off-balance, Nate tumbled, and Johnny pinned him with his knees.

The others cheered.

"Kill him, Johnny!"

"Get him!"

"Hit him again!"

"Go, Johnny!"

Johnny socked Nate in the eye, which made Nate so mad that he worked free and punched Johnny in the mouth. Finally Anton grabbed each boy by an arm. "All right, break it up. Quit it, you two. Johnny, if you hurt him bad, there's gonna be big trouble."

Johnny jerked away from Anton.

"I'd never tell on him," Nate snapped.

"Let's go," Anton said to the others.

They headed toward the field, all except Johnny. Nate looked at him with fury, and Johnny glared right back. Nate's eye ached, and he could feel it starting to swell.

Johnny spat blood. "I bet you don't have a dead mother, either," he said sulkily. "Or a stepmother. Or a brother who likes to beat you up."

"I got all those," Nate replied.

"Is Nate even your real name?"

"Yeah."

There was a long silence.

"So, where you been the last couple weeks? Too scared to face me?"

"No, I wasn't scared of you. I had to go to the shore. I didn't want to, but I had to. And I just got back last night."

"You didn't want to go to the shore? What kinda stupid rich kid are you?"

"I didn't want to go because I liked hanging around with you. And I wanted to play the Lattimer game."

Johnny waited to answer. "We lost."

"Yeah?"

"Ten to eight."

"Too bad."

Johnny's lip was all puffed out.

"That hurt?" Nate asked.

"A little. Your eye?"

Nate shrugged. Johnny took out his tobacco and bit off a chaw.

"It was my father's idea," Nate said at last. "I didn't have a choice. And I didn't know ahead of time."

"Boy, Nate." Johnny shook his head, allowing himself a slight grin. "When I saw you standin' there with the boss of all bosses, I thought I was dreamin'."

Nate didn't reply.

"You should've told me," Johnny said. "From the start, I mean. Why'd you lie?"

Nate was embarrassed to admit the reason. But if he had any chance of staying friends with Johnny, this was the time for the truth. He took a deep breath. "When I was at boarding school, I—"

"What's boarding school?"

"It's school you live at."

"Live at a school?" Johnny asked, puzzled. "Away from your family?"

"Yeah."

"*You* did that?"

"Yeah, since last September."

"How come?"

Nate shrugged. "I was getting in trouble a lot. My father and I, we don't get along. He was sick of having me around."

"So he sent you away?" Johnny asked, dubious.

Nate nodded.

"You come home on weekends?"

"No. I was home for Christmas, though. For a week. And a week at Easter."

Johnny just stared.

"Anyhow, at school, I didn't have any friends. So I got to know some fellows in town. I *thought* they were my friends. After I got kicked out, my father—"

"Kicked out? Of school?"

"Uh-huh."

"How come?"

"I had a bad fight with one of my teachers, and I was expelled. Well, other things, too, but that was . . . the last one."

Johnny nodded slowly.

"When I came home, my father—"

Johnny broke in again. "Where is this school, anyhow?"

"New Jersey. You know where that is?"

"Yeah. How'd you get home?"

"By train."

"You went on a train? All by yourself?"

"Yes."

Johnny looked skeptical—as if taking a train alone at their age was harder to believe than working in a breaker. "Go on," he said.

"Anyway, I thought those fellows were my friends. But then the headmaster told my father in a letter that I *had* no friends. That they only liked me for my money. So when I met you, at first I was afraid that if you knew who I was, you'd only like me because of my money. But after a while . . . I was afraid you'd *hate* me because of it."

Johnny turned his head, frowning deeply.

"Well," Nate said, "I better go."

"Yeah" was Johnny's only reply.

Nate hauled himself to his feet and started off.

"Nate?"

Nate turned.

"I'd've liked you either way."

"But why?" Nate couldn't help but ask what he'd wondered for so long. Other boys fell into two categories: the ones who didn't know he existed and the ones who hated his guts. What made Johnny different?

Johnny grinned. "Because you didn't back down when I said I'd run you off. And you let me ride your bike. And after that"—he shrugged—"everything else."

Nate was aware of trying to smile but not quite being able to. "I better go," he said again.

And again Johnny replied, "Yeah."

But just as Nate reached the bike, Johnny called his name and trotted over to catch up with him. "Come tomorrow," he said.

Nate felt a rush of hope.

"Let me talk to Anton and Emil," Johnny added. "Anton was wishin' we had you for the Lattimer game. And we're supposed to play them again. But I don't know if they'll take you back. Things have changed, see. At the colliery."

Nate frowned. "What do you mean?"

"Well . . ." Johnny looked toward the field. "I don't know if I should say. I gotta talk to Anton and Emil. But come tomorrow, awright?"

"All right."

"See you!" Johnny yelled, running off.

"So long."

Nate watched him go. Johnny made a detour and picked up his glove.

28

NATE WAS ANXIOUS to know what Johnny meant about things changing at the colliery. But Tom had already left for Alice's mountain house, and Nate wasn't about to ask anyone else in his family. Pa believed his story about crashing into a tree; Anna only stared. By morning the eye was purplish blue, but Mary seemed satisfied that her ice and towels had brought down the swelling.

When Nate got to the ball field, everyone was sitting in the weeds, waiting, though he had purposely arrived late. His stomach knotted up as he searched each grim face.

"Anton and Emil say you gotta answer some questions," Johnny said solemnly.

"I'll answer whatever you want."

"Siddown," Emil snapped.

"You shut up, Emil," Anton said. "I'll tell him what to do." He turned to Nate. "Sit down."

Nate sat.

"Why'd you start coming here?" Anton began.

Johnny broke in. "I told you. He came—"

Emil swung his arm back, hitting Johnny in the chest. "He can *talk,* Johnny. I heard him with my own ears."

Johnny said nothing. Nate saw him swallow hard.

"I was riding my bike," Nate said. "I met Johnny picking huckleberries. He asked me if I wanted to play baseball. And I did."

"You some kinda infiltrator?" Emil asked. "Like McParland?"

Nate shook his head, baffled. Who was McParland?

"Your family send you here to find out what's goin' on?" Anton demanded.

Nate said, "I—I—"

"He doesn't know what you're talkin' about!" Johnny protested.

"Johnny, shut up!" Emil said sharply. "You're the one brought him here! Maybe we oughta be askin' *you* a few more questions!"

Johnny spat tobacco juice and glared at Emil.

"I *don't* know what you're talking about." Nate glanced from Anton to Emil and back again. "My family send me? I'm not even allowed to go *near* the breakers or the patch towns. If my father knew I came around here, he'd kill me. They *don't* know I play with you. They *don't* know I know you. I don't know who McParland is, and I don't know what you're talking about!"

Anton jerked his head toward Emil. They stepped away from the group.

Mikey said to Nate, "McParland—"

"Shut up, Mikey!" Anton yelled. "You don't, *none* of you, say a word to him!"

Nate caught Johnny's eye. Johnny winked without smiling. Anton and Emil appeared to be arguing, but at last they nodded at each other and returned.

"Tell him who McParland was," Anton said to Johnny.

"You know who the Mollies were, right, Nate?" Johnny asked.

"Everybody knows that," Nate mumbled.

"Well, McParland was the guy who got them hung. He was a Pinkerton agent, came to the patch pretendin' to be a regular miner. He got in good with 'em, then turned 'em in. And they got hung."

"Okay," Nate said after a moment. "But what's it got to do with all of you? Or me?"

Emil and Anton looked at Johnny.

"I *told* you!" Johnny said. "He doesn't know!"

"You don't know what's goin' on at the collieries?" Anton asked.

Nate shrugged. "Only what you fellows said, that day. About the union. We don't talk about business at home. Heck, we don't talk about *anything*."

"Is that the truth, Nate?" Anton asked, fixing him with sincere eyes.

"It's the dead square truth, Anton."

Again Anton twitched his head. Again he and Emil conferred. Then they walked up to Nate. "Get on your knees," Anton said.

Nate's eyes darted to Johnny. Johnny nodded in reassurance. Nate raised himself to one knee, then the other.

"You gotta swear your loyalty," Emil told him. "Make the sign of the cross."

"He ain't Catholic," Johnny said.

"Well, what is he, then?"

"Presbyterian," Nate said. "But I know the sign of the cross." With all the Irish in their house, he ought to know it well enough.

"Then make it," Emil ordered.

With the first two fingers of his right hand, Nate touched his forehead, then his chest, left shoulder, and right shoulder. Wouldn't Mary be amused to see this!

"All right," Emil went on. "Your mother's dead, Johnny says?"

Nate nodded.

"Then you swear on your mother's grave that if you ever betray any breaker boy or any other miner, you'll burn in hell."

"I swear," Nate said without hesitation.

"No—*say* it," Emil growled.

Nate said deliberately, "I swear on my mother's grave that if I ever betray any breaker boy or miner, I'll burn in hell."

"Okay," Anton said.

Nate's sigh of relief was followed by a clicking sound. He lifted his head: a jackknife blade glinted in the sunlight. He tried not to be scared. But it was him Anton stood over with that knife. What was he planning to do with it?

"Johnny." Anton handed Johnny the knife. "Get up, Nate."

Johnny pushed up his own shirtsleeve and nicked the underside of his forearm. The cut was fast, efficient—Johnny didn't even wince. Blood bubbled up on his skin. "Hold out your arm," he told Nate.

Blood brothers.

Nate had heard of friends becoming blood brothers, but he never thought it could happen to him. When you had a blood brother, the two of you stuck together no matter what. One would die before he'd harm the other. Nate pushed up his sleeve and offered Johnny his arm.

Johnny squinched his eyes. "Go ahead," Nate urged, and Johnny nodded. But his hand was shaking when he pressed the knifepoint to Nate's skin, then bore down harder and gave a little pull. Nate's blood oozed, but he was too happy to care about the pain.

As Johnny pressed his cut to Nate's, all the boys gave a cheer—except for Emil.

"Okay, Anton. Now *tell* him," Johnny said.

Anton said to Nate, "You swear . . ."

"Anton!" Johnny barked. "Tell him or I will!"

"The strike's started," Anton said. "It's happenin' in McAdoo, and it'll come here. When it does, we'll shut down every colliery in the county."

Nate looked into Anton's angry eyes. His attitude had sure changed since the subject last came up.

"You swore on your mother's grave," Emil warned him.

"I know what I swore!" Nate shot back.

"Your grandpa doesn't like it, see," Emil said contemptuously. "He doesn't like unions, workers gettin' together to fight for their rights. He just wants men to take what he dishes out, and take it, and take it, and take it."

That didn't sound like Grandpa, with his slippers and whiskey and chess games. Nate started to say so. But then he remembered the shouts in the library—*This is still my business, Thomas! Do not presume to tell me how to run my business!*—and he shut his mouth.

"Well, we're done takin' it," Emil continued. "The fight's about to start."

"Shut up, Emil," Anton said. "There ain't gonna be no violence. We'll just shut 'em down, and if they want to ship any coal, they'll *have* to deal with the union and make some changes."

"Yeah!"

"Damn right!"

"Shut 'em down!" everybody agreed.

"What are the changes they—you want?" Nate asked, and the grumbling stopped.

"We want a decent wage," Anton explained. "Fifteen percent more. We want them to lower prices in the company store. And we don't want to have to use the store at all, if we don't want to."

"Tell him about the tax," Emil muttered.

"The operators are makin' us all pay a new tax, just because we're foreigners. The alien tax, it's called."

"Really?" Nate asked.

"Yeah, and it ain't fair and we don't want to have to pay it," Mikey said.

"Well, what if they won't?" Nate said. "My—all the operators. What if they won't deal with the union?"

Emil spat tobacco juice. "They got no choice."

Nate couldn't imagine Grandpa or Pa or his uncles or any of the other operators in a situation where they had no choice. No choice was for breaker boys. No choice was for Nate.

"It still might work out," Anton said, and Emil gave a snort of disbelief. "It might," Anton insisted. "And I'm done talkin' about it. Who came here to play ball?"

"Me!"

"I did!"

"Yeah!"

The boys ran for the field.

"Bobby, shortstop," Anton ordered. "Luka, right field. Nate . . . third base."

Nate played, ran, and shouted, but his heart wasn't in the game. Was it true what they'd said about this new tax? Could he find out if he read Pa's newspapers? The boys had taken him into their confidence, and Nate wished he could do the same. But he would have been embarrassed to tell them about the railroad companies, like vultures on the fence. Nate's family had so much, how could the breaker boys ever believe they feared losing it? More to the point—why should they care?

29

The fight's about to start . . . We'll shut down every colliery . . . They got no choice. Nate heard the words again and again as he lay in bed—or rather, on it. Heat rises, that much he knew, but why did every bit of it have to rise right into his corner of the house? He watched the big fan turning lazily above his head. It was useless against the stifling mugginess. Sleep was out of the question.

Maybe he should try the porch. He picked up his pillow and went quietly down the two flights. At least he *thought* he was quiet. As he reached the front hall, Pa's voice came sharply: "Who's there?"

Nate turned. Pa's study was lit, the door partly open.

"It's me, Pa," he said, showing himself.

Pa was at his desk, holding a pen. He looked rumpled and hot and unhappy. Papers were scattered everywhere. "What are you doing, Nathan?" he said with annoyance. "It's after midnight."

"I thought I'd sleep on the porch. My room is too hot."

Pa stroked his mustache. "Yes, I imagine it is." He stretched and yawned. "Go on, then."

Nate paused. Did Pa's working so late have to do with the fight Emil expected? Perhaps Pa would let something slip, as Grandpa had. "Are—are you busy, Pa?" he ventured.

"Yes, Nathan, I'm busy," Pa said impatiently, pressing his thumb and forefinger against the corners of his eyes. "I'm much busier than a man ought to be at this hour, so if you don't mind . . ." He waved Nate away.

" 'Night, then, Pa," Nate said, but Pa didn't answer.

Nate lay on a chaise longue, plumping the pillow under his head. His house, with its big windows and electric fans, seemed unbearably hot. How bad was it at Johnny's? Surely Johnny was sleeping on the porch, too, looking at the bright stars and the waxing moon.

Blood brothers, and yet Nate had no idea what it was like to be Johnny, living in a tiny wooden house, sleeping with a boarder, spending days in the noisy, filthy breaker.

So Nate had been inside the breaker—big thing. He had watched for all of ten minutes. He couldn't know what it was like to sit there hour after hour, breathing that air, picking slate, deafened by the racket.

An idea began to flicker. It was a spark at first, like a fire just catching, but it grew brighter and fiercer with every moment. Nate opened his eyes wide, as if watching it burn. He had seen the breaker only on Pa's command—entered when Pa brought him in, left when Pa took him out.

Now he would go in on his own terms, not to watch Johnny, but to do what Johnny did, to feel what he felt. To work by his side. He would walk up those steps not as a Tanner, not as the son of the boss of all bosses, but as Johnny's friend.

And if Pa found out, what of it? Pa made his contempt clear at every turn; Pa could hardly bear to look at him. Just now, for daring to show his face, for having the audacity to speak, Pa had shooed him away like a fly. So why should he care what Pa thought? What worse could Pa do than ship him to England, anyway?

Nate had been tense and angry every day since Pa had forced him into the breaker, but now he felt calm, even pleased. He closed his eyes and smiled.

Tomorrow, he would be a breaker boy.

30

THE BREAKER WHISTLE BLASTED Nate from a fitful sleep filled with dreams of running: through school corridors; down mazelike staircases; along dark, narrow passageways he had always imagined were in the mines.

Waking was no relief. As he remembered his plan, fear rose in his throat and pounded in his veins—but did not dampen his determination. If only he could get out of the house, it would be all right.

Stealthily, he crept up to his room and dressed, carrying his shoes back down. Not even Mary was up. Should he leave a note? *Back at dinner. Nate.* Why bother? Most likely no one would even notice that he was gone—except for Mr. Hawthorne, who would probably just be annoyed at the waste of his time.

Nate walked barefoot across the soft carpet of lawn and

put on his shoes in the carriage house. As he pedaled through the service gate, the only sound was the slight squeak of the bicycle chain.

Out of sight of the house, he gasped, then laughed with relief. But he must be quick; it was almost time. He imagined Johnny's surprised face. What would Johnny say?

When Nate reached the top of the patch, the miners were leaving their houses. Up the road they trudged, silent and sleepy, in ones and pairs, with sons and without, unlit mining lamps on their heads, tin lunch pails clanging against their legs.

Nate straddled his bike and waited. He got questioning looks, but no man said a word. As the breaker boys spotted him, they gathered around, bidding their fathers and brothers goodbye.

"What you doing here, Nate?" Bobby asked, trotting over. "Where's Johnny?"

"Hey, Nate, ridin' in your sleep?" Mikey said with a grin, punching his arm.

"Johnny coming?" Nate asked.

"What's *your* business?" Emil sneered, eyeing him with distrust.

"I'll say when Johnny gets here."

Andre came, and Luka, and Anton, and finally here was Johnny, looking puzzled, almost afraid. "Nate! Whatta you doin' here?"

"I want to go with you," Nate said, fixing his eyes on Johnny's.

"Go where?"

"I want to do the work. I want to go with you."

"Aw, no," Johnny said, shaking his head. "No no no no no no no."

But Emil jumped right in: "He can take Andre's place. They're the same size."

"No no no no no," Johnny continued, but everybody else took up Emil's side with shouts of approval. Mikey pulled Andre's cap over Nate's head, and Bobby tied Andre's scarf around Nate's neck.

"Give him your lunch pail, Andre," Emil said. "You take his bike."

Andre reached for the bike, but Johnny grabbed it, shouting, "No! It's a bad idea!" He pushed the bike at Nate. "Go home, Nate! Come back later! It's a bad idea!"

"No, he *should* come in," Emil said. "Let him do it. Let him see."

The others backed Emil up: "The boss won't know!"

"It'll be fun!"

"Come on, Nate!"

A man shouted in Polish—Johnny's father, far ahead, gesturing and waving.

Johnny called back to him, then mumbled, "Start walkin'." They all did, in silence, until Johnny said angrily, "He can't do the work."

"He'll learn," Emil snarled. "Just like the rest of us."

"What if they find out?"

"He don't mind takin' that chance, Johnny. So what do you care?"

"'Cause I don't want him to get in trouble."

"But I want to go," Nate told him. "I want to see."

"You already saw."

"I have to do it myself."

Anton had been silent. Now Johnny turned to him and pleaded: "Anton?"

"Let him come," Anton said, solemnly appraising Nate. "I think he can take it."

So Nate got the overalls and the lunch pail, and Andre rode off on the bicycle. They headed for the breaker at a trot. Andre's hobnail boots felt stiff and heavy.

Johnny panted instructions. "Keep your head down. Pull your scarf over your mouth. The boss won't look at your face, he never does. You'll sit by me. Do it how I do. Oh, God. The slate is shinier than the coal. Just pick it out and toss it. Oh, I don't like this. I don't like it at all." As they ran, Johnny cursed—long, worried oaths in Polish and English.

At the colliery yard, Anton slapped Nate on the back. "Good luck."

"Thanks."

Anton headed to the cage that would take him down below.

"Stay behind me," Johnny warned Nate as they climbed the rickety steps. "Do exactly what I do. Mikey, stick right by him. Bobby, stay on his other side. Oh, God, I don't like this one bit." Johnny continued to mumble and swear, and then they were inside.

It was oddly quiet. The boys lined their lunch pails against the wall and went to their board seats. Almost in unison they stuffed tobacco into their mouths. Johnny held some out to Nate. He refused with a grimace.

The boss, who was prodding coal chutes with his stick, ignored them. The man at the top waved, though, and the boys shouted to him. The machinery awoke with a tired groan and began to spit coal.

At first it wasn't too bad, and the boys seemed a lot less miserable than the last time Nate was here. When the boss turned away, they whipped slate at his legs. He paid no attention. Maybe the boys and the boss alike acted more serious and stern whenever Pa was around.

The boys didn't slack off, though. They were busy every moment. But their work was so familiar, they could do it while causing trouble. Nate quickly saw the difference between finger motions for picking slate and for talking.

Johnny elbowed Nate, nodding at his chute. It brimmed with coal. He must look less, work more. When the boss wasn't watching, Johnny reached over to help. He made a revolving motion with his hand: *Faster. Faster.*

Then Nate began to cough. He coughed so hard and long that he worried he'd keel over from breathlessness. Johnny offered tobacco again; this time, his eyes insisted.

It was the vilest thing Nate had ever put in his mouth, so disgusting that his eyes teared up. But it stopped the coughing. He tried to copy the others, lifting the scarf to spit juice on the floor—but his tongue felt swollen and tingly, too big for his mouth, and every time he tried to spit, he ended up swallowing some of the juice. Then his stomach heaved and his mouth watered. Surely he would throw up, right in the coal bin.

When could he get out of here? Why had he come? The

machinery's head-breaking clatter, the crashing coal, the suffocating heat, the choking dust, this repulsive chaw. What was he thinking? How could he have imagined he was made of strong stuff, like the breaker boys?

You think your life is so terrible? Here in the lap of luxury? Pa dragging him here, Pa looking at him last night as if he could barely stand the sight of him: *Yes, Nathan, I'm busy. So if you don't mind . . .*

Nate bent to his chute with a grim and angry determination, but . . . *He can't do the work.* Johnny was right. Nate pushed his cap back and rubbed his sweaty forehead with the back of his black hand. How did they keep these caps on all day, and these scarves over their faces? He was too hot, his back ached, he was about to vomit.

How long till lunch? He had to get out, breathe fresh air, drink cool water. Maybe Andre would come with his bike. Nate would trade back, admit he couldn't do it. Then wouldn't Emil be pleased?

Emil. Looking so scornful as he said, *Let him do it. Let him see.* Emil had hated him from the very start, and even more now that he knew who Nate was. *He* should *come in.* Yes, the only reason Emil wanted him to work was to see him make a fool of himself.

A grinding metallic screech made Nate's teeth hurt. The machinery thumped to a halt.

"All right, which one o' ya . . ." the boss began, brandishing his stick. The boys cheered, swarming up steps and down, as the boss trudged over to investigate.

"What happened?" Nate asked.

"I fixed it," Johnny said. "Nate, you look sick. I'm gettin' you out of here."

"No." Nate shook his head. "I'm staying."

Without another word, Johnny began to clear Nate's chute while the others roughhoused and shouted and cursed. Bobby and Mikey were among a group who hung out of windows. Now the boss had Luka by the ear, tugging him up to the top of the breaker.

"Luka did it?" Nate asked.

"Nope. But he's gotta clear it," Johnny said without looking up.

"How come?"

"Smallest hands."

"Isn't it dangerous?"

"He'll be awright."

The boss pointed with his stick. Luka knelt and stuck his arm right into the works.

"Havin' fun, *Nate*?" It was Emil, standing over him.

In reply, Nate pulled the scarf from his mouth and spat tobacco juice. Emil laughed, turning away. The breaker shivered back to life, the coal rattled down, and the boys scurried to their benches.

Right around then, Nate's fingers started to hurt.

At first it was just an irritation, a mild burning on his thumbs and forefingers. But soon every fingertip was on fire, and he wanted nothing more than to put them in his mouth like a baby. Each time he touched the slate, the pain seared through him, making his eyes fill with tears. What was this? How could he continue? What on earth was he going to do?

Johnny gave him the "Faster!" motion; Nate set to work. But surely his fingers were bleeding? He brought them close to his eyes. No blood. When he could stand it no longer, he did put them in his mouth, two at a time, tasting coal and something else. Like something from the science lab at school.

School. Spending hours in the library with Mr. Hawthorne seemed an extravagant luxury. At this moment, he could be stomping around reciting "Gunga Din." *You will do your work on water, / An' you'll lick the bloomin' boots of 'im that's got it.* Now he truly understood those lines. He would, no doubt about it, lick boots for water. Yet there must be hours till lunchtime.

He bent his head and picked slate—and conjugated Latin to take his mind off the pain. *"Sum, es, est; sumus, estis, sunt,"* he muttered. *"Eram, eras, erat . . ."*

When Johnny worked his legs backward to bring down the coal, Nate followed, reciting the names of the Seven Hills of Rome. When Johnny stretched his legs out to stop the flow, Nate did the same, mumbling: *"I was chokin' mad with thirst, / An' the man that spied me first / Was our good old grinnin', gruntin' Gunga Din."*

Johnny laid his hand on Nate's back. Nate turned, and Johnny gave him a questioning look. Nate nodded and reached gingerly into the chute. If only he had gloves, or a cold, wet cloth to wrap around his fingers. *"Dico, dicis, dicit,"* he said. *"Dicimus, dicitis, dicunt. Dicebam, dicebas, dicebat; dicebamus, dicebatis, dicebant."*

When the lunch whistle blew he scrambled to his feet, but dizziness sat him right back down. Then Johnny had his arm, and lugged him to the door. Outside, Nate couldn't get the tobacco out of his mouth fast enough.

Everyone crowded around vats of water with tin cups from their lunch pails. Johnny elbowed Nate to the front, and Nate drank gratefully.

"You did real good, Nate," Johnny assured him. "Okay, you can go home now."

"He can't go nowhere," Emil hissed. "The boss thinks he's Andre, and Andre ain't here."

"Well, I say Andre just got sick. And he had to go home."

"Oh, yeah?" Emil shot back. "And how 'bout when the boss docks him?"

"You think Nate can't pay him?"

"I'm going back," Nate interrupted. "I'll finish what I started."

The boys wolfed down sandwiches, fruit, and pie. When they saw that Nate had no appetite, they ate Andre's lunch for him. Then they ran wild as Nate watched in wonder, imagining a swimming hole.

"You get used to it," Johnny explained gently. "It ain't so bad after a while. Really."

Nate nodded. "What about this?" He turned his palms up to show his fingers.

Johnny drew breath between his teeth. "Redtop. I cried for a week. My mother rubbed goose grease on my fingers when I got home."

Home. Nate's heart skipped at the word. What would he do when he got home, covered in coal dust, with redtop fingers? He hadn't thought this through at all, just run off

doing something stupid again. Right about now Pa was sitting down to lunch, questioning Anna. Nate could see that
dining room as if he were in it. The looks, the silence, and
at last an explosion. Or maybe Pa would save that for him.

"Why don't you wear gloves?" Nate asked.

"Not allowed," Johnny said. "They say if you wear gloves,
you can't tell the difference between coal and slate." He
shrugged. "It's true. Slate feels smoother, don't it?"

Nate nodded.

"But the redtop goes away after a while."

"Where's Anton?" Nate asked.

"Oh, you don't come out for lunch when you work below. You eat down there."

Nate nodded again, and propped his chin on his fist.

"Nate, you sure you're all right?" Johnny said doubtfully.
"You don't have to finish, you know. Nobody'll think bad of
you. Hell, I—"

"I'm staying."

"Okay," Johnny said. "Awright."

The afternoon was even slower and more torturous. Nate's
head ached from the racket, his back from the hunched-up
sitting. Now, in addition to the redtop fingers, his eyes
burned with coal dust. He picked, and picked, and picked—
but never fast enough.

A sharp blow fell across his shoulders, shooting pain up
his neck and down his arms. He dared not meet the boss's
eyes, but the boss tapped his stick on Nate's bin: *Faster.* Then,
for good measure, he whacked the backs of Nate's hands.

Nate saw the white-hot light that meant he was losing control. He started to get up. This was just about enough. He'd reveal who he was and tell this lout of a boss that he'd have him fired for his brutish behavior, and then he—

No. Wait.

Heavily, Nate sat back down. If he did all that, it might make him feel better for a few seconds. But it would surely make life miserable in the long run. More important, it could make life miserable for his friends. Did he really have the power to have the boss fired? Not likely. And if the boss, and then Nate's family, found out that the boys had brought Nate into the breaker . . . Nate looked at Johnny, whose forehead was creased into a curious frown. Johnny turned his hand like a wheel: *Faster. Faster. Faster.*

31

"You did great, Nate!"

"You stayin' for baseball?"

"Wait till we tell Anton!"

"I thought he was gonna thrash the boss!"

Nate weaved as he walked, and Johnny put an arm around his shoulders. "Come to my house, Nate. My mother will take care of you."

Nate shook his head. Something told him that the sooner

he got home, the better off he'd be. And besides, if anybody else's mother touched him right now, he would surely cry for his own.

Andre returned with the bike, as planned. They changed clothes in the woods, but Nate knew that did little to improve his appearance.

"Thanks, Nate," Andre said. "I had a great time!"

"Oh, yeah; me, too," Nate managed to joke.

Everyone laughed—even Emil.

"You be okay?" Johnny asked, his eyes clouded with concern.

"Yeah," Nate answered.

"Hey," Emil said.

Nate turned.

Emil thumped him on the back. "You did all right."

"Thanks," Nate said.

But as he rode away, he felt too sick to be proud.

Nate approached Hazleton woozily, with no idea of what he'd do when he got there. It hurt to grip the handlebars, so he tried to steer with his palms. He was desperate to be home—in his bathroom, then in his bedroom, door locked. But many human obstacles remained, and those inside the house weren't the only ones.

What if Grandpa's carriage passed him? Or the carriage of just about anybody in Hazleton? Who might see him from the trolley? On the street? He rubbed and rubbed at the coal dust. There wasn't one person in all of Luzerne County who wouldn't know in a second what it was, and wonder how he'd come by a face full of it.

He had to get to the creek and clean himself, or try to. But before he could take that plan further, he stopped for another reason. He was definitely going to throw up. He wheeled his bike off the road, then ran into the underbrush, falling to his knees. Every time he thought he couldn't possibly be sick anymore, his stomach heaved again and the stench of tobacco juice filled his nostrils.

Finally, he rocked back on his heels and sat, holding his aching head.

That was when he felt a shadow over him—and looked up into Patrick's grim green eyes.

"What've y' been at, lad?" Patrick demanded. "What've y' done?"

Nate's instinct was to leap up and run, flying fast and far, into the thick weeds and bushes. Instead, he turned up his palms, showing Patrick his fingers.

"Jesus, Mary, and Joseph." Patrick sat heavily beside him. "What in the name of the Savior? How? *Why?*"

"I had to know. What it was like. My friends . . . work there."

"Friends?" Patrick's voice rose high with surprise. "In the breaker? *You?*"

Nate nodded.

"Ah, Lord, what'll we do now?"

We? The word shocked Nate to his heart's core. He could not answer.

Patrick pulled out a handkerchief and rubbed at Nate's face, holding his chin. "Y'r father'll murder y' if he knows where y've been. Murder! They've been lookin' for y'. Wouldn't y' know?"

"I—"

"Sent me out, y'r da did, and I finally spotted *that* thing." He waved his hand toward the bicycle. "Now how're we t' get y' into the house, that's the question. And cleaned up proper."

"I—I—"

"Well, if we're caught, we're caught. I'll fetch y' to Mary, she'll know what t' do with y'." He put the handkerchief away. "Come on, then," he said briskly, standing.

Nate got up, trembling with dizziness. "Patrick?"

Patrick looked at him.

"I'm awful sorry about what happened," Nate said haltingly. "Back at Easter. What I did, I mean."

"Aye, it's easy enough to apologize to someone who's helpin' y', isn't it?" Patrick said grudgingly as he started off.

"But I am," Nate persisted, following close. "And I have been since it happened. Only . . . too proud to say."

Patrick stopped short at the bike. "Lucky I've got the brougham today. Thought there'd be a thunderstorm, with all this heat." He scratched his head. "I'll put you and it inside. Take the back way. Come in through the service gate. And pray." He muttered as if talking to himself, then resumed walking. Nate rolled the bike behind him.

"Right, in with y'. Lord forgive me, I feel a common criminal."

Nate tugged while Patrick pushed. It was a tight fit, but they got the bicycle into the carriage.

The bumpy ride over dirt roads made Nate feel even more nauseated. The heat inside the brougham was stifling. He lay on the velvet seat, with his head hanging over the side. If he got sick again, it would not be pretty. He held his cap under his mouth, just in case, and mumbled, "Please, please, please."

When the carriage-house roof blocked the sunlight, he sat up slowly, carefully.

Patrick lifted the bike out, and Nate climbed down. "Stay here," Patrick ordered. "I'll see if the coast is clear."

"Pat?"

"Aye?"

"You haven't said," Nate mumbled, looking at his shoes, "if you'll accept my apology." He felt as if all his blood had drained into his aching fingers. He lifted his hands awkwardly in front of his chest, trying to ease the pain.

Patrick took the back of Nate's hand in his own big, rough palm. " 'Tisn't just the sharpness of the slate, y ' know," he explained, inspecting the fingers. "Like you might imagine. It's the chemicals from the blastin' of it that give a boy redtop."

"Johnny—he's my friend—he says it goes away in a while."

Patrick nodded. "That it does." He released Nate's hand. "I accept it," he said, and turned away.

"Mother of God!" Mary breathed, clutching at Nate's arm. "Oh, Blessed Virgin and all the saints!" She hustled him up the back stairs, Patrick on her heels. "We'll be sacked, Pat, sure enough, if they find out we know!"

They piled into the servants' bathroom. Mary shut the door and folded her arms as she eyed Nate critically. "Just *look* at the state of y', now! What's this foolishness!" She ran a bath. "Y'll have to bathe here, and then it's me who'll be scrubbin' out the coal grime, I suppose."

The water reminded Nate of his desperate thirst. He twisted the cold-water tap, cupping his hand to gather some to his mouth. But the water stung his fingers, so he stuck his mouth directly under the faucet, drinking greedily.

"Telephone to Mr. Tanner's office, Pat; say we've got him." As Patrick left, Mary continued, "Y'r father'll kill y', Nathan, if he knows what y've been at."

Nate stopped drinking just long enough to say, "So I hear."

"Strip off those clothes. Surely that's not what y' wore in the breaker?"

"No, I changed clothes with a friend."

At that she went quiet, and at last she said slowly, "Oh, of course. Oh, she was on to y' after all. She'll figure it out now, for sure."

It wasn't hard to guess who "she" was. Nate said nothing.

"Strip down and get in that bath." Mary sounded like a drillmaster. "We've got to get y' in bed before any of 'em gets home. Mrs. Tanner's out inquirin' after y', and poor Tory, too, worried sick. But *I* knew y' were up to no good, I just *knew* it! We'll tell 'em y're ill."

"That won't be much of a stretch," Nate muttered, kicking off his shoes.

"And those fingers, y'll have to hide 'em. Goose grease, that's the thing for it. I'll get some while y're bathin'. Undress y'self, I said, Nathan!"

"Not with you here!"

"Ah! I saw what y've got when y' were five years old!"

"Well, I'm not five anymore," he grumbled. He tried to unbutton his shirt, but the effort shot pain through his fingers. "Mary?" She turned; he held up his hands. "I can't."

She shook her head, taking over the task. "Honestly, Nathan, what gets into y'? Workin' in the breaker! What d' y' mean by that?"

He shrugged. "It's where my friends go. I wanted to know what it was like."

"An' *how* did y' meet these friends?"

"Riding my bike. Down by Harland."

"*Harland!*" she nearly shrieked. "Great God and little fishes! Y' mean to tell me y've been in *one of y'r family's breakers?*"

There was a soft knock, and Patrick came in.

"Oh, Pat, did y' know? It was Harland he was in!"

"Jesus," Patrick said, sliding his hand over his face.

"What if somebody saw y'?" Mary demanded.

"I had a cap on. And a scarf. But you know what I learned, anyhow? None of the adults even look at you."

Mary and Patrick exchanged glances. She turned off the tap and then, without consulting Nate, she unbuttoned his pants. His face burned. He said nothing. "Be quick," she said softly. "Pat and I'll be just outside."

Nate sank gratefully into the tepid bath, hearing the comforting sounds of Patrick and Mary murmuring on the stairs.

He tried to keep the sponge in his palm as he scrubbed his neck, face, hair, arms. Wash it all away. Pretend it never happened. A whole new set of lies.

"Are y' decent?" Mary asked, tapping on the door.

He wrapped himself in a towel. "Yes. I couldn't get the plug out," he said sheepishly when she entered.

She reached in and yanked it; her arm emerged from the bathwater coated with a black film. "Pat and Fiona have got the stairs covered. Sneak up there in the towel, get into pajamas, and hop in bed. I'll send something to eat later."

"Okay."

"But first, hold out y'r hands." He obeyed. Mary scooped something from a jar and gently rubbed it into his fingers. It was cold and soothing.

"Mary?"

"Hmm?"

"Thank you."

"Y'r welcome," she said, looking into his eyes. "Run along."

32

NATE WAS PREPARED to accept his punishment for staying away all day, not telling anyone, and missing his tutoring. He was prepared to take the consequences if Pa found out he'd worked in the breaker.

But he was not prepared for what did happen.

Pa knocked at a quarter to eight, saying quietly, "Nathan?"

"Yes, Pa." Nate buried his hands beneath the sheet.

Pa stepped in, shut the door. He didn't seem angry, although there was an odd expression on his face. Nate had seen it before, but when?

"They tell me you're not well," Pa said, tentatively approaching the bed.

"No, Pa."

"I—I would have come sooner, but Tory peeked in before dinner and said you were asleep."

"I suppose I was."

It was strange to have Pa in his room. Had Pa ever been here before? Stranger still, Pa actually sat on his bed. "Nate," he said wearily. "I shouldn't have lost patience with you last night. I was tired. And concerned about business. But I needn't have taken it out on you. When you ran off, I felt responsible. And awfully worried, son. The weather was so hot, I thought . . . I feared you'd gone swimming."

Nate couldn't bear Pa's being kind. A thrashing would have been more tolerable by far. Worrying about him, calling him "son." And all at once Nate remembered when he'd last seen that look of Pa's: at Mama's funeral. Then the whole day crashed down on him, and he turned his back on Pa to face the windows.

"I don't blame you for being angry," Pa said, standing.

He was leaving? Already? "I'm not," Nate choked out.

"You're not crying, are you?" Pa said with quiet disapproval. "Nathan?"

"No, Pa."

"You're much too big to cry, aren't you?"

Nate nodded, and took a deep breath that sounded, in his own ears, an awful lot like crying. Embarrassed, he squeezed his eyes shut and pushed his face into the pillow.

"Listen, Nate, I've been thinking." The tone caused Nate to look up. Pa adjusted the lampshade. "I've been thinking a great deal, and Mother—Anna—and I have been discussing it. Would you like to attend school here in Hazleton this fall?"

The room tipped and whirled. Had he heard right? "Here? But what about England?"

"England!" Pa hooted. "What's England to do with anything?"

"Fred said you were sending me to school in England."

Pa burst out laughing. "Oh, he did, did he? Well, that sounds like the sort of trick I'd have played on Uncle George when we were boys! But how could you believe such a story, Nathan?"

Let me count the ways, Nate thought, but held his tongue.

"England, for heaven's sake," Pa said, shaking his head. "I admit to inquiring into schools, though none so far away as that! But you've done well this summer, despite the unpleasantness regarding the shore. I thought we'd try keeping you at home, if it's agreeable to you."

Agreeable? Not to go to another dreadful boarding school, allowed home only two weeks a year? Agreeable to stay in his own room, while Fred went off to prep school? It seemed like a dream—but the dream would fade to dust if Pa learned about today.

"Nate?"

"Yes, Pa. I'd like to stay."

"You seem awfully grim."

"It's just that I don't feel well."

"Shall I telephone to Dr. Walsh?"

"No!" His voice came out so sharp, he startled himself. Then he said calmly, "No, I'll be all right. I'm stomach-sick, is all. I probably ate too many huckleberries."

"Ah, huckleberry season! I remember it well! We'll see how you are in the morning, then. I'll let you get some rest now."

"Okay."

Pa patted his head. It felt stiff, mechanical, as if Pa wasn't quite sure how to do it. "Good night, Nathan."

"'Night, Pa."

When Pa clicked the door shut, Nate scrunched under the sheet. He'd been steeling himself for another year of sharing a room with boys who hated him, of having no one to eat with in the dining hall, of teachers despising and humiliating him. But . . . stay home? Surely not. Anna, for one thing. She'd kept away all evening, and that wasn't like her. *She was on to y' after all. She'll figure it out now.* Surely she'd figure it out and tell Pa; then so much for school in Hazleton.

There was only one possible solution: he'd have to stop going to the patch and the baseball field. If he lay low and stayed in town, perhaps nobody need ever know what he'd been doing all summer—and especially what he'd done today.

With a sigh, Nate reached up to switch off the light. Yes, he'd have to keep away from the breaker boys. At least for a while.

33

NATE HID HIS FINGERS along with his secret. At mealtimes he was especially wary, positioning his hands carefully, resting them in his lap between bites. And he visited the kitchen often for goose grease.

Yet the boredom was far more painful than the redtop. In the afternoons, when the breaker whistle sounded, he longed to ride to the ball field, hear the raucous greetings, see Johnny's welcoming grin. Johnny was probably worried that Pa had caught him. Nate thought of asking Patrick to go to the patch and tell Johnny what had happened. But Patrick had already done enough for him. Whenever Nate felt tempted to go himself, he focused on dormitories and dining halls and Fletcher.

This year things would be better. He'd try harder to behave. When Anna had been his governess, she'd attempted to comfort him after fights with other boys: *You mustn't be so easily bothered, Nate. If you ignore the teasing, they will stop.* And Headmaster had said, *Why must you react to everything? Why can you not shut your ears and open your fists?* That was easier said than done. No one understood why he was always angry, not even he himself. But if he'd been able to control his temper after being whacked by the breaker boss, he ought to be able to control it in school. Well, he'd get the chance to prove it soon enough. The term would start in about a week, right after Labor Day.

Labor Day. What was going on with the union and the strike? Pa was out at meetings every evening, or at Grandpa's house after dinner. Tom was still away with Alice and her family. Nate tried to read the newspaper, but the stories were more confusing than enlightening. And Nate could find nothing about this new alien tax. He put the papers aside; it was all too complicated. Soon Tom would be home, and Nate would ask him.

One afternoon, as Nate made his way down from his bedroom, he heard Martin's whine from the day nursery. "You've got to wait," Lucy replied.

"I not *wanna* wait!"

"Young man . . ." Lucy warned him.

Nate pushed the door open. "Wait for what?"

"For James to wake up; then we may go outside," she explained.

"Dat not fair, Nayfin!" Martin's brow was furrowed, his lower lip thrust out.

"Well, where's his mother?" Nate said.

Lucy lifted her eyebrows disapprovingly.

Nate sighed. "Can I take him out?"

Martin clutched Nate's leg. "Pweeeeze, Wucy? Pweeeeeze?"

At last she smiled. "Will you look after him carefully, Nathan?"

"Yes," Nate said wearily.

"All right, then."

Nate brought the chattering boy through the kitchen. Why on earth had he gotten himself into this?

"What're *you* up to?" Mary asked with delighted surprise.

"Don't ask," he grumbled, and she laughed as he ushered Martin outdoors.

But it was pleasanter than he had expected. They played wheelbarrow, Nate holding Martin's ankles as Martin walked along on his hands. They played catch with a big red ball. Maybe for Christmas he'd get Martin a baseball glove.

When Anna arrived, they were feeding the goldfish. "Aren't you nice, Nate!"

Nate wasn't sure "nice" was quite what he wanted to be. "Martin didn't feel like sitting inside, waiting for James to wake up," he explained. "But, uh, I've got to go now. Pa said I'm to get a haircut."

"Yes, I know, but I was wondering, dear. I don't want to impose, but would you mind taking Martin along?"

"Martin? You mean get him a haircut?"

Anna laughed. "Not exactly. Let him watch. I'm thinking of having his cut soon."

Nate looked at Martin's flowing curls. Yes, it was definitely time.

"Perhaps it would do him good to see his big brother have a haircut," Anna continued. "In case he might be afraid when it's his turn."

Nate held back a scowl. Playing with Martin on the grounds for a while was one thing. Taking him into town was entirely another. "Well . . . all right."

"Good. Do you hear that, Marty, darling? Would you like to walk with Nathan to the barbershop, where big boys go to have their hair cut?"

"Yes!"

"Now, you *must* hold Nate's hand. Nate, promise me you'll hold his hand every moment."

"All right."

She pressed a fifty-cent piece into his palm. "Afterwards, why don't the two of you have some ice cream."

Terrific. Now it was a festival. But he mumbled "All right," and took Martin's hand. "Come on."

"Stay with Nate, Marty!" Anna sang out.

"Yes, Maaa."

Martin's bored tone made Nate smile. He gripped Martin's hand a little tighter as they walked off the grounds.

34

"Hey! Is Nate!"

Nate looked up in time to see Bobby get clouted on the head by Johnny. Then they were facing one another: Nate and Martin going west on Broad Street; Johnny and Bobby and Mikey walking east.

"Hi, Nate!" Mikey said.

"How you doing?" Bobby said.

"Shhh!" Johnny hissed, poking their backs.

"Hi," Nate mumbled, casting furtive glances right and left. "Hi, Johnny."

"Hi, Nate," Johnny said with a peculiar grin.

"What—" Nate shrugged. "What're you guys doing here at this hour?"

"You mean you don't know?" Mikey asked.

"We go on strike!" Bobby said proudly.

"Nayfin." Martin tugged his hand impatiently. "I want ice cweam!"

"Hold on a second," Nate told him. "On strike?" he whispered. "You are?"

"Why you don't play ball?" Bobby asked.

"Shut *up*, Bobby!" Johnny swatted him.

Again Nate surveyed the surroundings. "Will you fellows be in town a while? I can talk after I . . ." He held up Martin's hand. "I have to take him to Jacobs'." Johnny gave Nate a questioning look. "Martin," Nate replied, then added, "my little brother."

Johnny nodded, breaking into a wide grin. "Meet us in Memorial Park?"

"Okay," Nate agreed. "After I take Martin home."

They walked on.

"We on stwike!" Martin repeated. "We on stwike!"

Nate winced. "Uh, Martin? Do you know what a secret is?"

"Yes."

"Well, babies can't keep secrets. But do you think *you're* big enough to keep one? For me?"

"I not a baby!"

"I know, you're a *big* boy. Right?"

"Wight!"

"So, don't tell anybody about those fellows, okay?"

"Okay," Martin said agreeably, and pulled Nate ahead. "Come on, Nate! Wet's get ice cweam!"

When Nate entered Memorial Park, Johnny was alone, straddling a Civil War cannon. Nate walked past without a word, tipping his chin up as a signal for Johnny to follow. Partway down the Hazleton hill, Nate waited.

"What'd you do with Bobby and Mikey?" he asked when Johnny caught up.

"I ditched 'em. I wanted to talk to you alone."

"So. You're on strike?"

"We're all in the union now," Johnny said with a proud nod. "An' we went out a couple days ago. You got your day of work in just in time! Hey, how'd it go, anyhow? When you went home?"

"It was all right."

"Then why didn't you come around?"

"Well, my Pa . . . That night he said I've been so good, I won't have to go to boarding school this term."

"Really? You get to stay home? That's great!"

"Yeah, but if I get caught with you, the deal's off, you know?"

They walked in silence until Nate said, "I felt bad about not coming. And not letting you know. I *want* to play, but I can't take the chance. Not right now, anyhow."

Johnny wrapped an arm around Nate's shoulders. "Ah, that's awright. You didn't hear *my* side of it yet."

Nate looked at him.

"Uh, I hate to say it, but you couldn'a played with us, anyhow."

"What do you mean?" Nate asked, bristling.

"And it's my fault, too. That night, at supper, Papa and Stefan and Machek were all fired up about the union and the strike. And I got all fired up hearin' it, them goin' on against your grandfather and the rest of your family. And I— I— Well, I told 'em."

"You *told* them!"

Johnny screwed up his face. "Isn't that the stupidest thing you ever heard? I guess I thought they'd think it was funny. A Tanner workin' in the breaker. You know how funny Papa thought it was?"

Johnny turned and lifted his shirt. Nate drew a sharp breath: Johnny's back was striped from a whipping.

"Oh, it's better now. A *lot* better. But Papa said I can't ever play with you again."

Nate stared hard at the ground as they walked. "So, I guess your pa and ma hate me now."

"Well, no more'n your pa hates me."

They stopped and faced each other.

"My pa doesn't even know who you *are,*" Nate said, surprised to hear himself defending Pa.

"Yeah," Johnny said, nodding. "Exactly."

Nate turned his head quickly, feeling as if he had an orange stuck in his throat. "I better go."

"Nate, listen. Maybe we can't hang around anymore. But

we're still friends." Johnny showed Nate his blood-brother scar. Nate did the same. Both smiled, but just barely.

"Do you, um"—Nate shrugged—"need any money?"

"No, thanks," Johnny said shyly, and punched Nate's shoulder. "Maybe I'll see you sometime."

"Yeah." Nate could barely speak.

"Okay then. So long, Nate."

Nate waved and turned away, trudging up the hill. What did this mean to Johnny, really? He had plenty of other friends. But to Nate it was everything. Here he'd been thinking he'd chosen not to play with the breaker boys, that he could rejoin them any time he wanted. But he'd been so wrong.

A miner wouldn't let his son play with a Tanner.

Wasn't that a perfect ending.

35

MARY'S WORDS WERE CLIPPED and tight: "She's in the conservat'ry. Y're to see her right away."

"Mary?" Nate asked suspiciously, but she turned her back.

"G'wan. An' keep y'r temper. An' be respectful."

Martin. Again. Just when he was starting to like the rotten beast. Just when he thought Martin was starting to like him. His little brother. His little *brat*.

Anna didn't acknowledge Nate's steps on the tiled floor. He cleared his throat. "Mary said to see you."

She was spraying plants with a brass mister. "What's a secret, Nathan?"

"What?" he asked, to buy time.

Now she faced him. "Give me your definition of a secret, please."

"Anna . . ."

"Your definition of a secret, Nathan, if you please," she repeated sternly.

"When you know something and you don't tell anybody."

"Oh, very good. Precisely what I might say." She crossed the room to stand before him. "Now. Would you like to hear a three-year-old's definition?"

He stared at her.

"A secret is something you tell only one other person."

Nate dropped his head, squeezing his eyes shut.

Anna resumed her misting. "It was the word 'strike' that intrigued him. So at last, I pieced it together. This puzzle I've been working on all summer, not a very difficult one, but—" She shook her head. "I think I didn't *want* to finish it, really. I didn't want to see the full picture. I questioned them. The staff. They owned up to their part. I ought to have them all dismissed for such disloyalty to your father and me."

"If you—"

"Nathan, *don't*. Do not threaten me, do not make it worse for yourself. And don't blame Martin. He's three years old, and he adores you, Nate. He would never hurt you."

Nate walked to the French doors. "Well, now you won't have to put up with me. Go ahead and tell Pa, and he'll—"

"And I would never hurt you, either," she cut in, resting her hands on his shoulders. "How can I make you see that? I want you to be part of this family. I won't tell your father, but *promise* me you will not play with those boys again. Promise."

"I *can't* play with them again." Nate looked out at the garden, tapping his fingers on the window glass. "Johnny—he's my friend, the one I met first—he told his father who I am. And *his* father won't let him play with *me* anymore."

After a long silence, Anna said quietly, "It's best that way, dear."

"You mean that they don't get to know us? And we don't get to know them? So we can all keep our bad ideas about each other forever?"

"Well." Anna's voice was frosty as she stepped away. "This certainly doesn't sound like the boy I've known to show such scorn for servants and their place."

"Maybe I've changed. Wasn't that what everybody wanted? For me to change?"

She didn't respond.

"I guess this just isn't the right *way* to change, is it, Anna?"

"Oh, Nate." Anna shook her head sadly. "Will you never stop fighting?"

"I hope not." He opened the French doors. "I hope I never do," he said, and went outside.

36

A COUPLE OF DAYS LATER, Nate was in the third-floor hall when he heard voices from the billiard room. He approached quietly, and stopped short when he heard Fred's voice.

". . . delivered three hundred Winchester rifles to Mr. Fielding's office, and two hundred to ours," Fred was saying.

"Really?" It was Tom who answered.

"Yeah, you've been missing all the fun. And now I suppose we'll *both* miss the rest of it, with school starting Tuesday."

"Fun, huh?" Tom said. "You've got a strange idea of fun."

"Well, I admit it. I'd like to stick around and see those Hunkies and Dagos get put in their place," Fred said disgustedly. "I'd like to do the putting myself, but Pa says I'm too young to be one of the deputies, and he wouldn't let me join, anyhow."

Winchesters! Deputies! What could this mean? Heart pounding, Nate stepped closer to the open door, leaning carefully against the wall.

"But I'll tell you what," Fred continued. "You know how I've been saying all summer that I can't wait to get away from the coal?"

"Yes, you've made it *quite* clear."

"Well, I believe this whole mess has turned me around."

"Oh?"

"I'll stay in coal. When *I'm* in charge, you'll see those miners behave."

Tom snickered. "You sound pretty sure of yourself."

"I'm sure, all right," Fred replied. "It's too bad we leave Sunday," he went on. "I don't think anything will happen before Labor Day. Then they'll have their little rally and work themselves into a righteous frenzy about how awful we treat them. Next week is when it'll get really hot, is the thinking."

"I've got to admit," Tom said in a jovial manner, "I'm just as glad I won't be around for whatever—"

An arm reached around the doorframe, and Fred pulled Nate in. "You little sneak, why are you eavesdropping on private conversations?" Fred shouted, shoving him against the wall.

"Take your hands off him!" Tom yelled. Nate had never seen Fred look so shocked. "Let him go, Fred! What the hell do you think you're doing?"

Fred released Nate. "What's *he* doing creeping around—"

Nate interrupted him. "If you wanted privacy, you should have shut the door."

Fred glared at him, then stalked out of the room. Nate was trembling, from fear as well as surprise. Fred would get him now—and get him good.

"Hello, Nate," Tom said.

"Hi," he answered, trying to sound just as casual. "When did you get back?"

"A couple of hours ago."

"Did you have a good time?"

"Nathan, *were* you listening?" Tom asked firmly.

Nate nodded.

"Well, you shouldn't have been." Tom handed him a cue and set up the balls. "You take the first shot," he said.

Nate tried and missed.

"Nate, did you understand?" Tom's voice was low as he chalked his cue.

"Why do they need Winchesters?" Nate replied. "And deputies?"

"We're afraid the miners will become violent, or damage company property. In other counties, strikers have bombed collieries, burned breakers. And we just heard that some strike leaders over in Dubois were arrested for carrying revolvers and knives." Tom made his shot. "So the operators asked Sheriff Martin to deputize some men. To track the miners on their marches, and make sure things don't get out of hand."

"If Fred was a deputy, things *would* get out of hand, I bet."

"Fred"—Tom shook his head—"he makes it personal. As if he's got something against the miners. But we don't all feel that way. It's simply . . . It's business, Nate. Do you understand? We *can't* give in, just as I told you before."

Nate lined up his shot, but missed again. "Can't we give in just a little?" he asked. "And then maybe they'll give in a little, too?"

Tom sighed. "There's a word for that, Nathan, in the world of labor unions. It's called bargaining. And Grandpa just won't do it."

"But why not? What's so wrong with it?"

"Grandpa simply won't deal with anyone who doesn't work for him. And the union leaders don't work for him. He's said it for many years, Nate. And now he's an old man. He is not going to change."

Nate nodded, feeling worried and chilled. *No violence,* Anton had said. But Tom spoke of bombings and fires, revolvers and knives. Winchesters. Deputies.

Nate watched his brother line up another shot. Tom was the one person in this family who ever tried to explain things to him. Maybe he should tell Tom what he'd been doing all summer. Maybe if he told Tom the miners' side of things, Tom could figure out a way to help. He took a deep breath. "Tom, do you know about this tax we're making the foreign workers pay?"

Tom bristled. Giving Nate a severe look, he said coldly, "Tax that *we're* making them pay? Now who have *you* been listening to, Nathan?"

"I, um—I just—"

"Listen, Nate, here's the story on the alien tax." Straightening up, Tom thumped the cue against the floor. "It's this Fahy fellow and his so-called union who are responsible for it. The foreign miners blame us because they don't understand how Fahy stabbed them in the back."

"But why would Fahy do that?"

"Because he was trying to win the approval of the American miners, *that's* why. The Americans don't like the foreigners—they say they work too cheaply. The operators adamantly opposed the tax, but Fahy had it pushed through.

Then he shows his face here and they treat the hypocrite like a hero, a saint!" Tom was practically shouting now as he furiously chalked his cue. Just like Anton—in June, so calm and reasonable, but now . . .

"The tax *will* be overturned, because it's clearly unconstitutional," Tom continued passionately. "But in the meantime, who ought to pay it? Should the companies have to pay an unfair tax that was proposed and backed by the miners' union?"

"Um, no, I guess not."

"Say, Nathan, who *have* you been talking to?" Tom asked, frowning. "A shopkeeper? Some of them are—"

"No!" Nate said quickly. "No, I just—I don't know, I heard something somewhere in town."

Now Tom sighed and said ruefully, "Sorry, Nate. You asked a simple question and I jumped down your throat, didn't I?"

"It's okay," Nate mumbled.

"It's just that things are getting very tense, and we don't know where it will lead."

"All right."

"Is there anything else you're confused about?" Tom asked.

"No," Nate said quickly. "No, I'm all set." But he was sweating, shaking. He couldn't believe he'd been about to tell Tom his secret.

"Nate?"

He looked up. "Huh?"

"Your shot," Tom said with a reassuring smile.

When Nate returned to his room, Fred was in it, leaning against a window with his arms folded, grinning.

"Get out," Nate said, standing by the door, ready to run.

"Get out? Get out?" Fred said, feigning innocence. "Well, *gee*, Nate! If you wanted privacy, you should've shut the door!"

Nate turned. He'd make it down the stairs before Fred could catch him.

"Oh, *Naaay*-than."

Fred's taunting tone gave Nate a shiver. He looked back: Fred was holding up the soldier box.

"Give it," Nate said, diving across the bed. "Give it!"

Fred shoved the box behind him on the window ledge and grabbed Nate by the shoulders. "Does the wittle boy want his wittle soldiers?" he said in a whiny voice.

Nate tried to reach around him, knowing it was futile. "Give it, Fred!" he said through his teeth, humiliated to hear his voice tremble.

"Oh, are you going to *cry* now, little baby?" Fred shook him hard. "Are you going to cry good and loud so Tom will come and protect you again?"

Nate ducked his head, bit his lip.

"Yeah, you're so tough when Tom's there, aren't you? Well, you don't look so tough now. I believe you *are* going to cry."

Nate inhaled deeply and lifted his eyes to his brother's. "Give it back, Fred. Please. Mama gave those to me."

Fred's face changed entirely. For a second, Nate thought *he* might start to cry. Then Fred shoved the soldier box hard against Nate's chest and slammed out of the room.

37

ON HIS LAST DAY of tutoring, Nate surprised Mr. Hawthorne with a present—and surprised himself by feeling sad.

"Why, thank you, Nathan," Mr. Hawthorne said, turning the blue enameled pen in his fingers. "It's very handsome. I shall always remember you when I write with it."

Nate wanted to say that nobody had forced him. It was his own idea, and he went to Meyer's and chose the pen himself. Instead, he asked brusquely, "Well, what'll you do now?"

"I leave for my new appointment."

"Where's that?"

"Lindenwood Academy. It's just outside Philadelphia."

"Are you glad about it?"

"Yes, I am. It's a very good school, and I like the way they do things. They call it a house system. I'll supervise a group of boys, and live with them. We'll take our meals together. It seems a tad more civilized than some other schools at which I've taught."

"Yeah," Nate said with a bitter laugh.

"And I'm pleased that it's near a large city. Yet there is a beautiful river nearby, and an enormous park. The school uses both a great deal."

"What'll you teach?"

"Your favorite subject. Latin."

"I guess it wouldn't be quite so bad if *you* were teaching it," Nate all but mumbled.

"Well, *thank* you, Nate," Mr. Hawthorne said, chuckling. "I believe that's as close to a compliment as I'm likely to get from you! Now, let's have 'Gunga Din,' shall we, start to finish, your best dramatic recitation." He opened Pa's drawer himself and solemnly handed Nate the leather strap, then sat back expectantly.

"All right." Nate stepped away. He cleared his throat, closed his eyes, looked at the floor. Then he lifted his head:

"You may talk o' gin an' beer
When you're quartered safe out 'ere,
An' you're sent to penny-fights an' Aldershot it;
But when it comes to slaughter
You will do your work on water,
An' you'll lick the bloomin' boots of 'im that's got it . . ."

Stanza after stanza, he recited flawlessly. He was sure of it. Mr. Hawthorne gave encouragement with nods and smiles. When Nate finally reached his favorite part, he paused to get himself into the proper somber mood, beginning quietly:

"I shan't forgit the night
When I dropped be'ind the fight
With a bullet where my belt-plate should 'a' been.
I was chokin' mad with thirst,
An' the man that spied me first
Was our good old grinnin', gruntin' Gunga Din.

'E lifted up my 'ead,
An' 'e plugged me where I bled,
An' 'e guv me 'arf-a-pint o' water—green;
It was crawlin' and it stunk,
But of all the drinks I've drunk,
I'm gratefullest to one from Gunga Din."

Then, whacking tables and chairs right and left with Pa's strap, he shouted:

"It was 'Din! Din! Din!
''Ere's a beggar with a bullet through 'is spleen;
''E's chawin' up the ground,
'An 'e's kickin' all around:
'For Gawd's sake, git the water, Gunga Din!'"

He dropped his voice, and the strap, for the ending:

"'E carried me away
To where a dooli *lay,*
An' a bullet come an' drilled the beggar clean.
'E put me safe inside,
An' just before 'e died,
'I 'ope you liked your drink,' sez Gunga Din.
So I'll meet 'im later on
At the place where 'e is gone—
Where it's always double drill and no canteen;
'E'll be squattin' on the coals

Givin' drink to poor damned souls,
An' I'll get a swig in hell from Gunga Din!
Yes, Din! Din! Din!
You Lazarushian-leather Gunga Din!
Though I've belted you and flayed you,
By the livin' Gawd that made you,
You're a better man than I am, Gunga Din!"

"Bravo, Nate! Bravo!" Mr. Hawthorne leapt up, applauding. "Excellent! Oh!" He clapped his hand to his chest. "That was truly inspirational! I think you should perform it for your entire family."

"Not a chance," Nate said, embarrassed but pleased.

"I *truly* think you've a future in the theater, Nathan."

"No. I know what I want to do when I grow up."

"And what's that?"

"I'll be in charge of the collieries." Nate put the strap back and shut the drawer. "Every last one."

38

TORY HAD PLANNED to take Nate to a Labor Day picnic at Hazle Park, but Pa would not allow them off the grounds. The foreign miners were rallying, he said, and there was no telling what they might get up to. Tory was disappointed;

Nate was secretly relieved. He hadn't been looking forward to trying to socialize with her friends. The boys Tory knew were nice and polite and proper. Being with them would have made him miss Johnny even more.

Mary had the afternoon off, but she told Tory and Nate she'd make up a basket so that they could have their own picnic, right here on the grounds. When Nate went to the kitchen to fetch the basket, he found Patrick there with Mary. Patrick was all scrubbed up, and Mary was wearing a crisp white shirtwaist and a hat with blue ribbons. There were two picnic baskets on the table.

Nate just looked from Patrick to Mary, in shock.

"Close y'r mouth, Nathan," Mary said. "Y'r tonsils are showin'."

"*You* two?" he asked.

Mary looked admiringly at Patrick. "Shall we tell him, Pat?"

"I've asked her to be my wife, lad," Patrick said, beaming. "And she's accepted—can't say I know why!"

"*You* two?" Nate repeated. "Since when?"

"Since a while," Mary said with a sly smile. She whisked one of the baskets from the table. "Y' just weren't payin' attention, now, were y'?"

Still in shock, Nate watched them leave. At the back door, Patrick turned and winked at him. Then off they went, arm in arm.

Everyone except the youngest children had been summoned to Grandpa's house that evening for "a family meeting about the situation," Pa had said. Nate knew it must be serious. They had never before had a family meeting—at least not in his lifetime. It was always just business, and always just the men.

When Nate walked in, Grandpa was sitting at one end of the long parlor, surrounded by his children: Pa and Uncle Henry and Uncle George and Aunt Louise, all with their wives and husband. Next came the grandchildren—girls in chairs, boys on the floor. The household staffs stood around the edges of the room.

The scene reminded Nate of something—but what? He avoided George and sat on the carpet near Mary and Patrick. Mary waggled her fingers in a little wave, and Patrick gave him a friendly nod.

"I've called everyone together on a matter of utmost importance," Grandpa began solemnly. "Children who are old enough to understand were asked to be present as well. And those of you who work in our homes were requested to attend because you are also part of this family. I trust each of you to act always in the best interests of my children and, especially, my grandchildren."

Nate turned around. Patrick was staring at the floor, and Mary looked worried.

"Of course you know of the troubles at the collieries. I believe the next few days will be crucial, perhaps even perilous. I want to state my position clearly, and let there be no mistake: I will *not* back down."

Nate's stomach tightened at the cold, angry words.

Grandpa's eyes were hard, his mouth set in a grimace. All at once, and for the first time, Nate could actually see him brandishing a sword as he led his troops at Gettysburg.

"These union organizers—these troublemakers who come between me and my men—who are they?" Grandpa's voice rose to a higher pitch. "Outsiders! They know nothing of my business, nothing of how we do things here! Men come here from foreign countries, and this family gives them a chance to improve their lot! If a man works hard, and his family along with him, they can build a worthwhile future! That's the way it's always been! It's how this country was made!"

Pa and Anna and the other adults exchanged uneasy glances.

"I was nearly ruined—ruined!—in the depression of '77, and I fought my way back from the brink of bankruptcy! And now these union agitators turn up and tell me how to run my business? How to deal with my men?" Rage shook the words. Grandpa slammed his fist on the chair's arm. "I won't have it! I fought one war for the Union, and the result of that war was that every man in this nation has the right to work for whomever he pleases! Now I'm fighting a war *against* a union—fighting for *my* right to tell *my* workers: If you do not care for the way I run my business, then *you* are free to work elsewhere!" He slapped the chair again. "I will *not* back down!"

Aunt Louise rushed to pat Grandpa on the shoulder. "Now, Pa. You must calm yourself. This is not good for your palpitations."

Grandpa sat back, breathing heavily.

Protect your king. Yes, that was it: a chess game, with Grandpa the king, surrounded by knights and bishops and rooks—and pawns.

Anna gave Nate a sidelong worried look, as if she knew about the frightening feeling inside him—the feeling of something building up, ready to boil over like a volcano.

"Well. Doubtless you will all hear plenty in the next few days," Grandpa continued somberly. "Some believe the operators ought to capitulate to these mob tactics. The *Daily Speaker*, for instance, clearly sides with the strikers. But we will stand firm: not a penny, not a *penny* more will they get while they are under the influence of rabble-rousing union organizers. If they—"

"Grandpa?" Nate was horrified at the sound of his own voice.

Every head turned, every pair of eyes stared.

"Nathan," Anna said in a ghostly voice.

"Nathan!" Pa barked.

"Nathan?" Grandpa asked with a puzzled frown.

"I was—I was wondering."

"Yes?" Grandpa said expectantly.

Nate took a ragged breath. "I was wondering if—if we treated them better . . . maybe they wouldn't think they needed a union."

As he and Grandpa locked eyes, there seemed to be no one else in the room. Grandpa looked hurt and confused and angry all at once, and he said in a level, threatening tone, "What did you say?"

"I've been in the patch," Nate answered. "And the company store."

In the hazy commotion, he stood up. He saw Patrick slide his big hand over his face. Without really meaning to, Nate walked toward Grandpa.

"I've been in a miner's house," he said. "I know how they live."

"Treachery!" Grandpa yelled, leaping to his feet.

Nate blanched, but he continued. "I know we don't make as much money anymore. But can't we give them just a little more? And do we have to charge such high prices at the company store?"

"Thomas!" Grandpa shouted, red-faced. "What is this?"

At Nate's side, Pa stammered "I—I—I—"

"In their houses, the rain pours right in through the roofs. Did you know? And they have rats."

"Nathan," Pa growled, grabbing his arm.

"And I've been in the breaker, Grandpa. I've done the work. I know what it's like to sit there all day, breathing that dust and listening to that noise." He extended his palms. "Your fingers—they get cut and swollen. And the boys chew tobacco to keep from choking. My friend's been doing it since he was ten. He doesn't go to school. He—"

"Enough!" Grandpa roared. He seized Nate by the shoulders, shaking him hard. "Do you know what we did to traitors during the war, young man? Do you?"

Of course he knew—traitors were hanged. Nate was stunned. How could Grandpa be treating him this way?

"Now, Pa." Aunt Louise scurried to Grandpa's side. "You must sit. Thomas, can't you control your son?"

"Let me be, Louise!" Grandpa continued, glaring at Nate. "Named for your great-grandfather! You side with *them* against your own family?"

"Because it isn't fair," Nate said, hearing the desperation in his voice. "It isn't fair."

"I'll disown you!" Grandpa raged.

Then two hands pried Grandpa's from him; two hands gently pulled Nate away. "Come, Nathan."

"Anna . . ." Pa's voice was steely.

"Thomas," she said firmly, "I am taking him home."

The next thing Nate knew, he was in an armchair, scratching his blood-brother scar. He didn't remember leaving Grandpa's house, or crossing the road. Anna paced the library, the fingertips of one hand pressing her forehead. "This is my fault," she murmured. "All my fault."

No, Nate wanted to say, *it's mine.* But he dared not speak.

The front door slammed. "Anna!" Pa barged in furiously, his eyes bulging. "Anna, how could you? How *could* you!"

"How could *I*?" Anna clapped her hand to her chest. "How could *you,* Thomas? Are you so afraid of your father? How could you not defend your own son?"

"He betrayed his family!" Pa shouted. "He must take what's coming to him, and you had no right to interfere!"

Misery covered Nate like a hot, heavy blanket. He had achieved the impossible—caused trouble between Anna and Pa. And he could never have imagined it would feel so bad.

"Thomas, when I married you, I promised to treat your children as my own. And that is exactly what I just did."

Pa tried to match Anna's calmness, but he sounded more cold than cool. "Thank you, Anna. Now please leave him to me."

"No."

Pa's exasperation rose again. "Anna, I'll deal with him as I see fit!"

"Fine, Thomas. But you'll do it before my eyes."

Scrunched in the chair, Nate was entirely drained of energy. His eyes darted back and forth, as if watching a tennis match. It was Pa's volley.

"Well, that suits me fine!" Pa stomped to his desk and jerked open the strap drawer. "I suppose I'll thrash him just as well with an audience! Nathan, on your feet!"

Nate got up quickly, to prove he wasn't afraid.

"Have you *anything* to say for yourself?" Pa asked, eyes smoldering.

"No."

Pa pointed in the direction of Grandpa's house. "Have you *any* idea of the trouble you've caused?"

"Yes."

Pa gave the signal. Nate placed both hands flat on the desktop, waiting for the strap's sting. It wouldn't be worse than the breaker boss's stick.

"I knew." Anna's words were deathly quiet.

Then, for an eternity, there was no movement or sound.

"What?" Pa said, befuddled.

"I knew what he had done. I was afraid to tell you."

"Then *you* betrayed *me*, Anna." Pa sounded hurt. Was that possible?

"I feared what you'd do to him," Anna replied.

Pa let the strap fall and dropped heavily into the desk chair. "Sit, Nathan. Please, Anna. Sit down."

Nate sat. Anna sat.

"Friends," Pa muttered. "Who are these friends, anyhow? Which breaker were you in?"

Nate shook his head, staring at the floor.

"Ah—not telling! More loyal to a bunch of foreigners than to your own family!"

"I don't want them getting into trouble because of me," Nate said. "It's not their fault."

"No, Nathan, it's not their fault," Pa agreed. "The blame for this situation lies squarely on your shoulders. But tell me, how did you happen to come by such friends? *That* is something I'd be very interested to know."

"I met them when I was riding my bicycle. I started playing baseball with them."

"So, let's see: I returned your bicycle to you. I allowed you the freedom to go where you wished. You chose to exercise that freedom by pursuing activities you knew I would have forbidden."

"They were nice to me," Nate mumbled. "They were my friends before they knew who I was—and after."

Following another long silence, Pa said, "There are many, many things, Nathan, that you do not understand. You are a child, and children should not involve themselves in their elders' business. You know nothing."

"I know what I saw," Nate said defiantly.

"Do something for me, Nathan, hmm?" Pa asked with a

slow, sarcastic smile. "Ask your 'friend' how he came to have a job in our breaker at the age of ten when the legal age is twelve. For the sake of expediency, I'll give you the answer: Their parents falsify the documents, Nathan. They all falsify the documents so that their children can work instead of attend school. Because of need? No, because they want to buy homes just as quickly as possible, and send money back to their relatives in whatever country they came from."

Yes, Nate remembered, that was just what Johnny had told him. But he wasn't about to admit it to Pa. And besides, there was Mikey, and Andre. "That's not always true," he said. "I know two boys, at least, whose families really need their pay."

"Yes, because their fathers spend every afternoon in the tavern," Pa said bitterly. "Clearing the coal dust from their lungs—isn't that the explanation they give?"

"Andre doesn't have a father," Nate shot back. "He was killed in a coal fall two years ago."

There was another long silence as Pa stroked his mustache. Then he said, "Well, Nathan, ask your friends, or their parents, or *any* of them, if they'd prefer to be back in Poland or Slovakia or Italy or Ireland. Ask Patrick. Ask Mary. Knock on any door in the patch. Ask them why, if things are so terrible here, they continue to bring more and more of their countrymen over to live and work."

Nathan said nothing.

"Every foreigner who comes to this country starts at the bottom and works his way up," Pa said, tapping hard on his desk. "But *these* people think, somehow, that they should have it easier! We've given them a chance at a new life, a better life—and now they expect a union to march in and make everything perfect for them! My father feels terribly betrayed by it. And now he feels betrayed by his favorite grandson."

Nate started: he, Grandpa's favorite?

"You doubt me, Nathan? When was the last time you saw your cousin George playing chess on Grandpa's porch? Or Tom or Fred, for that matter? But after this—" Pa shook his head. "I honestly don't know if he'll ever forgive you."

Nate ducked his head, blinking back tears.

"Oh, Thomas," Anna said sadly.

"There's no point in sugar-coating, Anna. He's got to understand the consequences of his behavior."

They sat in silence for a while, until Pa said scornfully, "You know what you saw. Well, what about all you don't see? Hmm?"

Was this another one of Pa's riddles? Nate didn't answer.

"When I was a little boy, my father left home every morning at six. Until five in the evening, he visited the collieries. He went underground every day. He knew each miner by name, he knew all their families. He helped them purchase land so they could build their own homes. Did you know, Nathan? He came home exhausted, had his supper, and then shut himself in his office until late at night. When the Civil War came, my father left his wife and five young children without hesitation to fight for his country. For four years, he suffered deprivation and illness. Dysentery. Typhoid. He fought all the major battles; I'm sure I need not list them for you. Before it was over, one of his children was dead, and his own health was ruined. Then he set to work and continued to build up his father's business. And when there was all the trouble with the Molly Maguires, his collieries were among the only ones that were not attacked—because of his reputation for fairness. Did you know *that,* Nathan? Hmm?"

"How would I know it, Pa?" Nate replied steadily.

Pa looked startled. He sat back.

"How would I know any of it?" Nate went on. "Did you ever tell me before? It's all a big secret. Shhh, don't talk about the coal. Not at the table. Not anywhere else. So how would I know?"

Pa shifted uncomfortably, and at long last he gave his response: "You may go, Nathan."

Nate walked to the door, then stopped. "There's a school near Philadelphia," he said. "Lindenwood. It's where Mr. Hawthorne's gone."

"What do you mean, Nathan?" Anna asked. "You're staying right here!"

Nate smirked without turning. He knew this family a lot better than Anna did. He was going.

"I'll look into it," Pa said, and Nate left the room.

39

"DON'T EVEN IMAGINE leaving the grounds," Pa told Nate. Breakfast was otherwise silent. Tory went glumly off to school with the twins. Nate was glad Tom and Fred had left for college and prep school. Fred would have sneered at him—and who knew about Tom?

Nate wished he could tell Johnny how he'd lived up to his blood-brother vow so that Johnny would know how important his friendship was. But Johnny probably didn't even care. Most likely, he'd forgotten Nate was alive.

Nate spent the morning wandering the house and grounds, trying to distract himself. Lunch would be excruciating, with just Pa and Anna. But there was no way around it. He would never give Pa the satisfaction of not showing up.

When he entered the dining room, Anna was already seated. "How *are* you, dear?" she asked.

"Fine, Anna, thank you," he said, and took his seat.

Pa strode in, dropping the *Wilkes-Barre Times* on the table. "Here you go, Nathan. Read it, since you thirst for knowledge."

Nate glared at him.

Pa tapped on the paper. "The one with the headline 'Strikers Close Four Breakers.'"

"No," Nate said evenly.

"All right, then," Pa said with false cheerfulness. "I'll read it to you. I'm sure it will interest Anna as well."

Pa seated himself and cleared his throat:

"It was a spirited meeting full of Italian and Hungarian curses, threats and insinuations. The line of march was hastily laid out. The marchers brandished pokers, bats, fence pickets, and small saplings. With a mighty cheer the column moved down the main street of McAdoo, where a Hun too tired to march sought seclusion in the cellar of his house. But the round-up ferreted him out and he was assisted into line on the end of eight clubs applied to his person in none too gentle a manner."

Pa looked up. "Translate that last part for me, please, Nate."

Mary was in the room now, serving.

Nate said through clenched teeth, "The man was forced to march."

"Beaten into it would be more precise, is that not correct?"

"That's what it sounds like."

Pa continued:

"Then with a cheer the army descended on No. 1 breaker. Down through strippings, over culm banks, through groves and over fields came the army of strikers like an avalanche. The breaker was won without a struggle, the enemy had fled.

"With a calm and determined step, the miners marched on to Hazleton. It was a grand and glorious sight; fully three

thousand five hundred strong. The captain of the police approached the strikers.

" 'Why do you come here? Disperse, you agitators of the peace.'

"The leader of the strikers replied, 'Get outta da way. We-a no stop!'

"The undismayed captain replied, 'Disperse or I'll run you in!'

" 'Ha, ha,' laughed the leader of the strikers as he pulled papers from his pocket. 'I am an Americano citizen. I defy you. We go through your city.'

"The brave captain, seeing the terrible power of the strikers, suggested that the police accompany the strikers to avoid conflict. The offer was accepted and the column moved again.

"It halted for a charge on the Hazle breaker. The deep-toned whistle announced the approach of danger, and the breaker miners vacated within six seconds.

"Victory! The strikers had again won the day. 'Twas a grand stroke to march eleven miles and close up four breakers. And as the setting sun cast its last rays over the distant mountain, the grand army of striking Huns, Italians, and Slavs marched to their homes to enjoy the calm and quiet peace after a day of war."

Nate gulped some water.

"So, Nathan," Pa said, "what do you think?"

What did Pa expect him to say? *You were right and I was wrong?*

"You've shown yourself to be a young man of principle—and very strong opinion. What do you think now?"

"I don't know, Pa." Nate trembled with rage. His hands, resting on the table edge, jerked up and down.

"You see, Nathan, there are two sides to every story," Pa said triumphantly. "Now, with their brute tactics, they've shut down four more breakers. Do you know how many collieries remain open in the whole of Luzerne County?" Pa held up a single finger. "One, and it's ours: Lattimer." He looked at Anna. "God only knows what's to happen next."

"Oh, Thomas," Anna said worriedly.

"May I be excused?" Nate asked.

"Eat your lunch," Pa ordered.

Nate's vision blurred as he got to his feet. "Pa, I'd like to be excused."

Pa looked him up and down. "Go."

In the kitchen, Patrick and Harry were having their lunch. "Nathan," Mary said quietly, and he stopped. "Y' know I have great respect for y'r da, but I must comment on something he just said to y'."

"*Mary* . . ." Patrick cautioned her.

"I've told y', Pat, I won't be shut up by you or anybody!" Mary whispered fiercely. "I've got something to say to Nathan, and I'll say it, by God!"

Patrick reddened, glowering at his plate.

"Y'r da told y' there's two sides to every story," Mary said. "But there are *three* sides to every story, Nathan. Y'rs, mine—and the truth."

Nate pondered, then replied: "The truth? How do you ever find *that*?"

No one answered. He went outdoors.

Tory tapped on the billiard-room door, startling him. "Sorry. May I come in?"

"Suit yourself," he said, expecting a lecture as he lined up his shot.

Tory ran her fingers nervously along the felt of the billiard table. "Everyone at school's talking about you."

"Terrific," he mumbled. The shot went bad.

"George and his big mouth. It's bound to get to the adults that he's blabbing it everywhere. Then *he'll* be in trouble."

Nate said nothing.

"Anyway, I think it's very brave, what you did. Going into the breaker, I mean. And then defending the boys to Grandpa. And Pa."

"Yeah, well, I think it was very stupid." His next shot failed as well.

"I know perfectly well you don't think any such thing," she said cheerfully. Picking up a cue, she chalked the tip.

He stared. "You play billiards now?"

"My friend's brother taught us." She giggled. "Better not tell Pa. I doubt he'd care for the idea!" She easily sank a difficult shot.

"And here I thought you were sipping lemonade and picking flowers all summer."

"That shows how little *you* know!" Tory said lightly.

"Yeah."

"Oh, Natey." She hugged his arm. "I haven't been much help, have I?"

Voices jumbled up in his head. Tory's: *You do make it so unpleasant* . . . Fiona's: *He's so nasty* . . . Anna's: *Always ready to push people away* . . .

"It's my own fault," he admitted. "You've been a lot nicer than I deserve."

"That is not true!" she protested.

"Uh-huh. It is." He slipped his arm from hers and chalked his cue.

"I think Pa's horrid to send you away."

"No, that's my fault, too. And besides, it's probably best right now."

"But you *hate* boarding school."

"I'll do better this year," he said, bending over the table. "I'm sure of it."

40

BY THURSDAY AFTERNOON, Nate's anxiety was at a peak. What were Pa's plans for him? What were the miners' plans for Lattimer? High in the copper beech, he gazed at the town. It seemed so peaceful that it was hard to believe there was a war of sorts going on.

Suddenly he blinked hard: Could that be Johnny there,

on the other side of the fence, walking along the sidewalk? The boy kept looking back at the house. Even though he was moving slowly, that jaunty walk was unmistakable. Johnny passed right under Nate's branch. Nate said nothing. Johnny continued to the corner, stopped, paused, then started back the way he'd come.

After Johnny had walked past the tree again, Nate climbed down and stood at the fence. "Johnny," he said. Johnny ran to him.

"Nate! Where'd you come from?"

Nate pointed up at the tree.

Johnny laughed. "I was hopin' I'd find you."

"Well, you did."

"I never saw your house so close up."

"Well, there it is."

Johnny furrowed his brow. "Whatsa matter, Nate?"

"Never mind," Nate said, shaking his head. "What're you doing here?"

"You mad at me for something?"

I'm mad because you're poor and I'm rich. Because we can't be friends. Because my family won't pay you more. Because the miners are carrying clubs, and my father made me listen to the story . . .

"No," Nate replied.

"You sure seem mad."

"Johnny. What're you doing here?"

Johnny studied his face. "I came to tell you about tomorrow. Because I want you to hear it from me. I want you to know—it ain't personal, it's business."

Just as Tom had said: *Fred makes it personal, but it's simply business.*

"What happens tomorrow?"

"Lattimer's the only colliery still—"

Nate interrupted him. "Yeah, I know all that. What about tomorrow?"

"There'll be a march," Johnny said steadily, still staring. "A big one. To Lattimer. To shut it down. The Italians there ain't in the union, but we're gonna get 'em in it."

"Oh, yeah? How? Beat them into it?"

"Whatta you talkin' about?" Johnny said defensively.

"It was in the Wilkes-Barre paper. That the miners beat men into joining the march. And carried clubs. Anton said there wouldn't be any violence. He said it was nothing like the Mollies."

Johnny's familiar grin returned. "So *that's* what you're mad about. Well, you shouldn't believe everything in the newspaper, Nate. They're all on the operators' side! Don't you know that?"

Nate looked toward the house. Was anyone watching?

"Those were no clubs, they were walking sticks!" Johnny went on.

"Pokers?" Nate said suspiciously. "Bats?"

Johnny shrugged. "Tree branches. Anything they could find. They don't have money for fancy, gold-tip canes like your grandfather."

Nate's throat tightened at the mention of Grandpa. "What about beating men to get them to join?"

"Well, maybe there's truth to *that*. Some fellows were just lazy. They're in the union, but they didn't feel like walking. But everybody's got to walk. That's the only way to show the operators we mean business. Ha!" He burst out with a laugh. "You shoulda been at Harland! Mikey's ma was beatin' her *own* husband to get him to walk. Otherwise he'd've stayed in the tavern all day!"

Nate allowed himself a faint smile. "Will you join this march?" he asked.

"No. They say you got to be fifteen." He shrugged. "I guess we'll go swimming."

Nate nodded. He wished he could go with them.

"I thought you'd be at school today," Johnny said.

"I'm going away to school."

Johnny's eyebrows shot up. "But your father said you could stay here!"

"Yeah, well, things have changed," Nate said bitterly.

"Tell me," Johnny coaxed him.

Nate wanted desperately to tell him. Not just about what had happened at Grandpa's, but everything Pa had said afterwards, and about Fahy and the alien tax, and Grandpa's point of view. But there was no time—and no point. The miners would believe they were right, no matter what. The operators would believe they were right, no matter what. "I have to go," Nate said. "If anybody sees me—"

"They know, don't they?" Johnny persisted. "You told 'em you know us, didn't you?"

"Yeah. I told them, all right."

"To try to help us."

"I have to go, Johnny." He headed for the house.

"Nate."

Nate turned.

Johnny stuck his arm between two of the iron fence posts. "Shake?"

Walking back, Nate gripped his hand.

"Take care," Johnny said.

"You, too. And tell—" He stopped. He had to leave now. "You know the sheriff has deputies. And they have rifles."

Johnny grinned. "A *peaceful* march, Nate. Not even any canes this time, Fahy's orders. This is America, Nate!" Johnny shrugged. "We got the right!"

"Yeah."

Johnny started off, then turned and retraced his steps. "If you can sneak away tomorrow, you know where to find us!"

"Okay," Nate said.

But he knew he wouldn't go. That was all he would need, to be caught with the breaker boys now. Pa would snap him up like a netted herring and send him to the strictest school he could find.

41

When Pa came in to lunch on Friday, he handed Nate a letter. Nate thought he recognized the handwriting. He opened it slowly, careful not to show any emotion.

Dear Nathan,

    I was surprised but delighted to hear that you will be joining us at Lindenwood.

The words swam. He felt a rush of joy and relief. Then he realized he was actually *smiling* at the letter. Was Pa watching? He evened out his face and read further:

    I am certain your father has told you that you will be living in my house, which I think will suit you. The boys are a pleasantly rowdy group, and the master isn't such a bad fellow himself.

    You will share a room with an agreeable lad called Timothy by his elders, Moth by his pards. I have just asked him what I ought to tell the new boy, and he responded: "To bring his baseball glove." I would add, don't forget your Wellingtons, as the boys seem to do a fair bit of mucking about in creeks.

    Don't fret over being the new boy. I have only begun to learn the ways and byways myself, so we shall be new boys together.

    Best wishes,

    Mr. Hawthorne

Nate folded the letter and laid it aside. "Thank you, Pa."

"You'd best start packing," Pa answered pleasantly. "Your train leaves on Sunday. And if you need to make purchases—coat, shoes, what have you—do it this afternoon."

Pa was telling him to go into town today, of all days? That was a comfort. Pa mustn't think the march would cause trouble.

Pa seemed relaxed all through lunch, eating with a hearty appetite, joking with Anna and Mary. Pa was probably glad to have the school plans settled, to be getting rid of him. Nate didn't even mind. He was just as eager to be away from this whole mess. Mr. Hawthorne's letter had worked like goose grease on redtop.

After Pa returned to work, Nate told Anna he was going to town to buy a new pair of Wellingtons. He didn't even try on his old ones first. He just wanted an excuse to wander around, and maybe learn what was going on. But as soon as he rode his bike through the gate, he saw people running along Broad Street toward West Hazleton. Without hesitation, he followed.

On the road below McKenna's Hotel, a crowd stood and silently watched. In front of them was a long line of deputies with rifles, and trudging up the hill were the marchers. How many? Nate tried to figure it out. When he was at Brock, he'd watched from his room as all four hundred students assembled in the quadrangle for field day. The group of strikers seemed to be about that size. At the head of the march, one man held an American flag.

As Nate got off his bike, he spotted Sheriff Martin, who was in charge of the deputies. "Get back, all of you!" the sheriff shouted to the spectators. "There's liable to be trouble if these men do not disperse!"

Nobody stepped back. Then the deputies began pushing the crowd roughly.

A burly deputy raised his rifle and looked through its sight. "I could get a bead on that fellow down there," he told another deputy, grinning. Was this his idea of a joke? Or was he serious? Again Nate recalled Tom's words: *He makes it personal. As if he's got something against the miners. But we don't all feel that way.*

Sheriff Martin walked toward the marchers, followed by the deputies. There were angry voices from both sides, but Nate couldn't hear what was said. Then one of the marchers bent over, reaching for something on the road, and in short order two deputies were pounding him and another marcher with gun butts. When the deputies were finished, blood was pouring down one striker's face.

Nate just stared, his heart in his throat. Another deputy grabbed the marchers' flag and tore it to shreds, and then a group of deputies and marchers were shoving one another until a shot was fired into the air—and everything stopped.

A man in a brown suit, but holding no rifle, quickly approached Sheriff Martin. The two argued, first with each other and then with the strikers' leaders. All at once, the trouble seemed to be over: deputies headed one way, marchers in the opposite direction.

The crowd of spectators broke up, too. "They didn't need to pound them like that," one man grumbled, shaking his head.

"Are you crazy?" another said. "Didn't you see that

Hunky was about to pick up a rock! He's lucky he didn't get shot!"

Their voices faded as they walked off, still arguing.

Nate approached a man who had been at the front. "What just happened?"

"The man in brown is chief of police in West Hazleton" was the answer. "He told Sheriff Martin the miners have the right to a peaceful march, but he told the strikers it would be too disruptive for them to go through Hazleton. They've got to go around West Hazleton if they want to get to Lattimer."

"Yeah, and the deputies are making sure *they* get to Lattimer first," another man added, nodding toward the trolley stop.

Nate looked: all the deputies were waiting for the trolley. A chill crept down his spine. Already there had been trouble, fighting, bloodshed—and a shot fired, even if only in warning. And that was just during a walk along the road. What would happen when the miners got to Lattimer and actually tried to shut down the colliery?

Maybe, Nate thought, he should warn somebody—go and find Pa, tell him what he'd seen. But would Pa believe him? Would he care? *What were you doing there?* Pa would say. *Go to your room. Pack your trunk. Stay on the grounds.*

Nate jumped onto his bike and pedaled quickly toward Harland.

42

"HEY, NATE! You came!"

"Johnny . . . Johnny . . ." Breathing hard, Nate bent over and hung his head, resting his hands on his knees.

"What?" Emil was the first one out of the water. He seized Nate's arm. "Trouble?"

Nate nodded. "Come with me, Johnny. We can get there first, if we hurry. You tell your father, get them to stop."

Johnny, dripping wet, was struggling into his clothes.

"What happened?" Anton asked, frowning. "Where are they?"

"They were fighting . . . the marchers and deputies. I saw it," Nate gasped. "Now they're heading for Lattimer. Come on, Johnny. Let's go."

Johnny did the pedaling first, with Nate on the crossbar. They switched back and forth from Harland to Hazleton. They did not speak. As they coasted into Lattimer patch, Nate could see the deputies, lined up in a crescent formation. A few of the strikers appeared to be in a scuffle with Sheriff Martin. The breaker whistle screamed—and the shooting began.

"No! No!" Johnny leaped from the bike. Nate gave chase, grabbing Johnny's shirt just before he got ahead of the bullets. "No! Papa! Stefan! No!" Johnny howled, fighting to free himself.

Strikers ran helter-skelter, toward buildings, behind trees, into the distance. But the deputies kept shooting. Nate watched through a haze of rifle smoke. *This is not happening. This is a dream.* His arms couldn't hold Johnny much longer. Would the gunfire never stop?

After a final, echoing blast, there was a ghostly silence.

Johnny shook himself loose and dashed toward the miners. Dazed, Nate walked forward. He must help them. He must do something. But what?

Moans of the wounded and dying rose in an eerie chant. Women poured from nearby Lattimer patch, shrieking and shouting in foreign languages. Some deputies skulked away, muttering to one another. Some stood with rifles by their sides, staring as if in shock. Still others began tending to the wounded.

Now Nate was in the midst of the fallen. Most of the unhurt marchers were running away, but a few had returned to help. What could he do? Here was a miner shot in the back, his shirt blasted to bloody tatters. Lying facedown in the dirt, he was still and silent.

Here one clutched his stomach, grunting as blood seeped between his fingers. "Oh, God," he groaned. "Oh, God."

'E's chawin' up the ground, an' 'e's kickin all around: For Gawd's sake . . .

"Get the water," Nate said, lifting his head. Where was the water around here?

Another boy rushed past, catching Nate's arm. "Come on!" He pulled Nate to a pump where a couple of tin pails lay. The boy pumped furiously while Nate held the pails. Now ambulances trundled up the road. And wagons. And hearses.

Someone said to the sheriff, "Sheriff Martin, how are you?"

"I am not well," he replied blankly.

Nate walked among the wounded, wiping faces with his wet handkerchief, holding a pail for those who could drink from it. Sometimes he tried to make his palms into a cup, but more water was spilled than drunk.

"Want to see wife . . . before die," one man said, sobbing, but Nate didn't think he'd get his wish.

Another man tugged at Nate's ankle. "Loose my suspenders, would you, young fella?" As Nate knelt to help, two men came with a stretcher and bore the man off.

All at once Nate was aware that he was sweating—and horribly hot. He rubbed at his wet face, then ran both hands through his damp hair as he looked around for Johnny.

A woman ran with a white sheet flying behind her. What was she doing? Stopping beside a man with a head wound, she frantically tore the sheet into bandages. A young man, bleeding from the arm, supported an older miner who'd been shot in the leg. They joined a steady stream of hurt men staggering toward a trolley.

Now Johnny passed, walking beside a stretcher. He did not notice Nate. It was Mr. Bartelak on the stretcher, eyes open, thigh shredded.

"Johnny!" Nate grabbed at his arm.

"He'll be awright," Johnny recited, no expression in his voice or eyes. "He'll be awright. He'll be awright." His pale face was streaked with tears.

"Where's Stefan?"

"Went for Mama."

"What about Machek?"

"He's okay."

Men loaded Mr. Bartelak onto a wagon. When the attendant tried to prevent Johnny from getting in, he lashed out: "Leave me alone! I'm going with him!"

"Yonny, Yonny," his father murmured.

"Go ahead," the attendant said.

Johnny scrambled up into the wagon and held his father's outstretched hand.

"I'll see you," Nate said, his voice shaking.

Johnny nodded.

Nate rubbed his eyes and returned to his work.

At last the dead and wounded were gone; the sounds of horses' hooves and trolley cars had faded away. Nate poured the remaining water over his aching head, dropped the pail, crossed the scarred road, and sat in the shade of a massive oak. Hunching over to hold his head, he was nauseated by the stench of his blood-soaked shirt.

"Hey." The other water boy sat beside him. "You all right?"

Nate nodded. "You?"

"Yeah. My name's Connie. What's yours?"

"Nate," he said, then forced himself to add: "Nathan Tanner."

"Tanner?" Connie's face clouded over. "What're *you* doing here?"

"That story's too long to tell right now," Nate answered, looking at the ground, but he could still feel Connie's eyes on him.

A man with a little notebook scurried up to them. "Who are you boys?"

"Who are *you*?" Connie demanded.

"I'm a reporter for the *Hazleton Daily Standard!*" the man said, clearly impressed with his own importance.

"And whose side are *you* on?" Nate asked bitterly.

"Side?" the man repeated. He pointed his pencil at Nate. "What's your name?"

"Leave him alone," Connie said. "Leave us both alone."

The reporter walked off, grumbling.

Nate knew he should go home; they would be looking for him. But he didn't move. If he stood, he might fall. "How many dead, you think?" he asked Connie.

"Can't tell."

Saying it—*dead*—choked him. He hauled himself to his feet and forced his voice to be steady: "Can I ride you home? I have a bike."

"No, thanks. I live right over there." He jerked a thumb toward the patch.

"See you, then."

"See you," Connie said.

Nate walked to his bike and picked it up. His feet felt like lead. He was pushing the pedals, but getting nowhere. *Faster. Faster.* He bit his lip. He did not cry.

As Nate approached the gatehouse, a policeman moved to block him.

"Let him be," Harry said. "He's Mr. Tanner's boy."

Harry tried to speak to him, but Nate kept moving. Sleep-walking. Yes, he must be sleepwalking.

By the back door, Pa was pacing in his shirtsleeves. Pa without a waistcoat! Nate had never seen Pa outdoors with no waistcoat or necktie. Never.

Then Pa spotted him, and began to run toward him. He'd never seen Pa run before, either. Clearly Pa didn't know how. Or had he just forgotten?

"Nathan," Pa said, reaching him. "Nathan, thank God!"

The sound of Pa's voice woke him, and Nate attacked. He punched his father as hard as he could while Pa, looking grim and determined, tried to grab his hands.

"They shot them!" Nate shouted. "They shot them in the back! The miners tried to get away, but they just kept shooting!"

You're not crying, are you, Nathan? You're much too big to cry.

"Why? Why?" Nate punched his father again and again till Pa finally succeeded in getting his arms around him, holding him close. Pa would get blood on his shirt. Imagine that—blood on Pa's shirt.

Nate struggled, sobbing, "Let me go, let me go, I hate you!"

But Pa held him all the tighter. "It wasn't meant to happen, Nate. You must believe me, this was not planned."

"They tried to get away." Nate choked out the words. "They shot them in the back. I saw."

"I'm sorry." Pa's hands were in Nate's hair, Pa's cheek against the top of his head. It felt so strange, so peculiar . . .

Nate buried his face in Pa's shirt, and let Pa hug him as he wept.

43

THE GOVERNOR had called out the National Guard, fearing that the miners would riot. From his bedroom window on Friday evening, Nate could just barely see the guardsmen setting up their camp in the fields behind the railroad station.

Everyone in the house treated him with great care and concern. He pretended he was fine, but he kept smelling blood, even when his clothes were in the trash and he'd scrubbed himself from head to toe in a hot bath.

There was no trouble on Friday night. After breakfast on Saturday, Pa was leaving for a meeting at Grandpa's when Nate caught up with him in the front hall. "Pa," he said, "may I ask Patrick to drive me to Harland?"

"That's out of the question, Nate," Pa said, not angrily, but without hesitation.

"I want to see Johnny, and make sure his father's all right."

Pa just stared at him. "Johnny, is it?"

"Yes, Pa."

"And his surname?"

"Bartelak, Pa."

Pa nodded. "I'll inquire after your friend's father. But this house is under guard, and you are not to attempt to leave." Pa put both hands on Nate's shoulders. "Do you understand me, Nathan? If the miners know who you are, they might harm you."

"They won't," Nate said.

"No, Nathan." Pa walked to the door, then turned. "Write your friend a letter," Pa suggested. "I'll have it delivered for you."

Dear Johnny,

I am sorry for everything. I wanted to come to your house and say it, but my pa won't let me. He's afraid if anyone knows who I am I might be hurt, but I know that would never happen. Anyhow, the house is under guard, so I have no choice. Pa said he will find out for me how your father is.

I wanted to tell you that I am leaving for my new school tomorrow on the three o'clock train. I hope the next time I come back here, things will be better. Please give my regards to your father and mother, Sofia, Stefan, and everyone else I know there. Tell them all that I am sorry.

Your friend,

Nathan Tanner

For the rest of the day, Nate and Tory and the twins stayed together in the drawing room, playing quietly and reading. The feeling in the house reminded Nate of the day after Mama died, when everyone spoke in hushed tones and the children found comfort in one another.

The twins kept asking Nate to tell what he had seen. He refused, even lied, saying he hadn't seen much at all. He didn't want to frighten them, or Tory, either. But he told Mary, and he told Patrick. He told them again and again. They listened kindly, nodding and frowning, at the kitchen table. It was so peculiar, how he had to keep telling it. Every time he repeated the same gruesome descriptions, he felt a little better, somehow, for a while.

At first he wanted to learn all the details, and he brought a stack of Pa's newspapers into the library and lay on the floor to pore over them, alone. Surely he'd be able to fill in the gaps of what he'd seen in order to piece together what had happened. But one paper stated that the miners "assaulted the sheriff" just before the shooting started; another reported that a wounded striker said, "The men were simply pushing their way through the line of officers when fired upon."

One headline called it a "Massacre," but another said it was a "Terrible Riot." Some papers referred to the miners only as "marchers" or "strikers," but others said they were "a mob," and one called them "raiders." Then another headline caught Nate's attention: "Conflicting Stories Told." With a bitter laugh, he pushed every paper away and stretched out on his back, rubbing his aching eyes. He knew that he would never learn what had really happened—not if he read every newspaper in the country, spoke to every person in the family and in Hazleton and in the patch towns. Everyone would tell conflicting stories, and they would all call their versions the truth.

Now the only thing Nate believed was what he'd seen

with his own eyes: No matter how or why the shooting began, some of the deputies *kept* shooting, even after the strikers had started to run.

44

On Sunday afternoon, Nate peeked in at the nursery door. James was already asleep, but Martin popped up in his little bed.

"Nayfin!"

Nate pressed a finger to his lips.

"I not *wanna* take a nap." Martin frowned.

"Shhh," Nate said, sitting beside him.

"You goin' away?"

He nodded.

"I not *want* you to go away."

"Well, I'll be back soon. Look."

Nate handed Martin a box. Martin opened it. "Sojers!"

"Will you take good care of them for me?"

"Oh, yes!"

Nate rubbed Martin's hair and stood. "Take your nap, all right?"

Martin lay down, looking solemn, cradling the soldier box. "Nayfin?"

"Yeah?"

"I wanna gib you a kiss."

Nate leaned over to let Martin kiss his cheek, then straightened up. "I've got to go." At the door he looked back. Martin gave him a little wave and a smile. Nate left, shutting the door with a quiet click.

He took the back stairs to the kitchen. When Mary saw him, she started wiping her hands on her apron. "I wish y' didn't have to go so soon, after all that."

"I don't mind. Really."

"Ah, Nate. She'd've been so proud of y'. And I am, as well. I'd hug y', if y' were mine. Ah, the devil! I'll hug y' anyhow!" she said, and squeezed him tight.

"Thanks," he mumbled. His arms hung awkwardly at his sides. Should he put them around her? No, that would be mawkish. He pulled gently away. "Um, Pa says I can come home for the wedding."

"That's lovely news, Nate. We'll want y' there, Pat and me both."

"Goodbye, Mary."

"G'bye, love."

On the porch, Pa and Anna were sitting with the girls. The twins rushed to Nate. "Which one am I?"

"What's *my* name?"

"Uh, you're Willie," he said, pointing. "And you're Minnie." Everyone laughed. He tapped one twin's head, then the other's. "Winnie. Millie."

"He got it!"

"He knows!"

"At last," Tory said, pressing his arm.

"I think he knew all along," Anna called from the glider.

"I'm not so sure I did," he admitted, approaching them. "I'll just say goodbye now, Anna."

Pa looked at his watch. "We've a bit more time, Nate."

"I know. But I want to go and see Grandpa."

Pa examined him, nodding slowly. Then he looked out at the quiet street. "All right. I'll be around with Patrick in a few minutes."

Nate reached for Anna's hand. When she gave it, he bent to kiss her. "Thank you, M—" He tried to force his lips to say the word, but his brain just wouldn't allow it. Blushing deeply, he told the floor, "I'm sorry."

"Oh, Nathan." She stood to embrace him, whispering: "I don't care what you call me. As long as you know I care for you."

"I do," he said quietly, and stepped away.

As Nate left the grounds for the first time since Friday, a clanging trolley pulled him back in his mind to Lattimer, where the wounded men had staggered toward the cars. A horse's hooves reminded him of a hearse, slowly bearing away the dead. And the leafy breeze sounded just as it had when he and Connie were sitting beneath the tall oak in stunned silence.

Nate stepped into Grandpa's drive. Never again would he be the boy who walked this way to play chess on a summer evening. Never would he hear Grandpa's war stories with the same ears. He tipped his head back. The sky was as blue as ever, but the smell of blood clung to him still. Four baths in two days—yet the sickening stench remained on his skin.

The big door swung open. Esther smiled nervously. "Why, Nathan!"

"Hello, Esther. I'd like to see my grandfather."

"Oh dear. I'm afraid—I'm afraid he doesn't want to be disturbed."

"You mean he doesn't want to see me."

Esther looked apologetic, but she neither replied nor admitted him.

Nate quickly edged past her. "Thank you, Esther, I'd rather hear that from him."

"Nathan!" She scurried after him toward the drawing room. He walked faster, feeling his heart pounding in his chest. "Nathan!"

Grandpa had the *Hazleton Sentinel* in front of his face. He did not put it down.

"I'm sorry, sir," Esther began. "He—"

"It's all right, Esther. I'm perfectly capable."

The icy voice chilled Nate's blood, but he stayed put. Esther shut the door behind her.

"I know you're angry," Nate said. "But I wanted to say goodbye."

Grandpa didn't so much as rattle the paper.

"I'm not sorry for what I did," Nate went on. "But I am sorry for lying all summer. And I'm not sorry for what I said to you. But I'm sorry I didn't say it in private."

Still no response. Nate walked to the door.

"Nathan."

Nate turned. The paper was on Grandpa's lap. He looked ill, and weathered, and very, very old.

"I'm a man of my time, Nathan, in every sense," he said slowly. "I find myself standing at the threshold of this new century as if . . . as if at the doorway of a party I've no wish to attend."

Nate swallowed hard and stepped closer.

"The union, this new breed of miner—I do not understand it." He shook his head, frowning. "We didn't ponder the possibilities, Nathan. We got caught out, and nineteen men lost their lives because of it. And I, for one, shall never forgive myself."

It isn't your fault, Nate wanted to say, but the words stuck in his throat as he watched Grandpa's paper tremble on his knees.

"You and I have the bond of old soldiers now, Nathan," Grandpa said with a grim smile. "We've both seen men killed in war."

"Will I ever be able to forget it?" Nate asked quietly.

But instead of answering, Grandpa said, "Come over here and shake your grandfather's hand."

Nate walked across the room and reached out. Grandpa's hand was big and warm.

"Off you go," he said in a gravelly voice, waving Nate away. "You'll do better this year, won't you, Nathan?"

"Yes, Grandpa. I will."

Pa was waiting in the brougham. "Well?" he asked when Nate climbed in. "Did he speak to you?"

"We spoke to each other," Nate replied.

45

"I HEAR Y'LL BE WATCHIN' me walk down the aisle," Patrick said at the station.

"I will. But are you *sure* you want to marry her, Pat? She's awfully bossy."

Pa laughed under his breath as Patrick blushed. "An' y're awful cheeky, ain't y'?" he asked, pulling Nate's cap over his eyes. "Well, lad."

"Thanks, Pat."

"Y're welcome," Patrick said, and thumped Nate's back before carrying his trunk to the platform.

Just then, Nate saw Johnny jogging toward him and Pa. He watched in shock as Johnny stopped short, took off his cap, and said, "Hi, Nate."

"Hi. Um—yeah, Pa, um—" He turned to stand at Johnny's side. "This is my friend, Johnny Bartelak."

"So." Pa surveyed Johnny from head to toe. "You work for me."

"Yes, sir. I'm in the Harland breaker." Johnny looked right back into Pa's eyes. "I got Nate's letter, and I wanted to say goodbye."

"You're the young man who took Nathan to work with you."

"It was his idea, sir," Johnny mumbled, turning red.

Pa nodded ponderously. "Does your boss treat you fairly, John?"

"Pretty fair, Mr. Tanner. He's awful quick with that stick of his, though."

"Hmm, well, we'll see about that. Now tell me, John, when you go underground, I suppose you wish to be a spragger?"

"Not me, sir," Johnny said. "I want to be a stable boy."

"A stable boy? Indeed?" Pa seemed amazed—as amazed as Nate was, listening to all this. "For heaven's sake, why would you *choose* to have dealings with those ornery mules?"

"Well, I like animals, sir. And the mules can be real nice, if you're nice to 'em."

Pa cleared his throat. "Well, then." He put his arm around Nate's shoulders in an awkward embrace. "I'll let you two have a private word. Don't miss your train, Nathan. Write to me tonight, would you?"

"Yes, Pa," Nate said dazedly.

"Goodbye, Mr. Tanner," Johnny said.

"Young man," Pa said in a pleasantly brisk manner. Then he walked away.

"Did that really just happen?" Nate said, feeling light-headed as he and Johnny started for the platform. "I can't believe he asked you so many questions. He never asks *me* questions unless he already knows the answers."

"He's not so bad as I thought he'd be," Johnny answered. "He's kind of nice, Nate."

Nate changed the subject. "I hear your father's okay."

"Yeah. He'll come home tomorrow. They say his leg will heal fine."

"What's it like in the patch?"

Johnny shook his head. "It's rotten, Nate. We lost some good men, and they all left widows and orphans."

Nate looked down the tracks. "You know they were arrested. The sheriff and deputies. There's to be a trial."

"Yeah, I know. You know the strike's over? We go back tomorrow. They gave us ten percent. And they'll make changes at the company store. It's a start, Fahy says."

"Well, that's good, but . . ."

"But what?"

"You still have to work in the breaker."

Johnny shrugged. "You still have to go away from your family."

"I don't mind so much."

"And I don't so much mind the breaker."

The train clanked into the station. "Phiiiiiii-la-delfya!" the conductor bellowed.

"Mama says goodbye. And Stefan, and Sofia. Everybody."

Nate toed the ground. "I thought they'd be mad at me. Especially your mother."

"She was, at first," Johnny admitted. "But she knows it's not your fault." He flashed a devilish grin. "She's still cursing your family, though."

Nate managed a smile. "Well . . . tell her I said *doeveed-zenya.*"

"You remembered!"

"Polish is no harder than Latin, I guess."

"Bawwwwwrrd!" the conductor hollered, then asked: "You boys going to Philadelphia?"

"He is," Johnny said, giving Nate a push. "*I'm* staying right here."

Nate climbed the passenger car's narrow steps and turned. "Take care, Johnny."

"Study hard, Nate," Johnny said solemnly. "So you can be the boss someday. Maybe you'll be the one to fix things."

"And maybe you will," Nate replied.

They both kept waving as the train huffed down the tracks. Johnny disappeared, leaving only his grin. Then that faded, too.

Nate lurched into a window seat, and the train began to rock him. For two nights he had stared at his bedroom ceiling, smelling blood, seeing horror if he shut his eyes. But in his new room, in just a few hours, he would rest. *Then we'll start fresh tomorrow.*

The coal breakers passed, scattered among culm heaps and patch towns. Banbury . . . High Ridge . . . Harland. Silent and still, they crouched like sleeping beasts, waiting to roar back to life, dreaming of morning.

AUTHOR'S NOTE

THE EVENTS OF SEPTEMBER 10, 1897, went down in history as the Lattimer Massacre. Nineteen coal miners were killed, thirty-nine wounded. The feared rioting did not take place; the mining community buried its dead with dignity and composure. Most of the coal operators made some concessions, and the strike was soon over.

Outrage over the shootings helped the union's cause. In the following months, membership in the United Mine Workers increased by fifteen thousand in the Pennsylvania coal region.

On February 1, 1898, Luzerne County sheriff James Martin and his eighty-seven deputies went on trial for murder. All were found not guilty by a jury of twelve on March 9.

Not surprisingly, newspaper editorials disagreed about the verdict. Some papers were outraged by it, believing the deputies had gotten away with murder. More often, the papers saw the acquittal as a triumph of law and order. Still, most expressed sympathy for the dead and their families, as well as hope that lessons learned on both sides would prevent similar tragedies in the future.

The *Philadelphia Record*'s observations of March 10, 1898, were perhaps the most trenchant and far-seeing:

But while Sheriff Martin and the deputies on trial with him
stand acquitted of deliberate murder, they cannot escape the
imputation of unnecessary slaughter. Whether as a result of
fright, panic or misapprehension can never perhaps be
certainly known, [but] the riotous strikers were shot down
without that degree of provocation which should immediately
precede and make necessary a resort to force.

The trial at Wilkesbarre was conducted with great
fairness. The charge of Judge Woodward was admirably clear
and impartial. Notwithstanding this, however, the result will
leave, we fear, unhealed animosities which only the lapse of
time can soften or obliterate.

By 1902, railroad monopolies had control of more than ninety-six percent of all anthracite coal lands. Most independent operators had been driven out of business; those who remained were locked into agreements that severely curtailed their profits.

Because *The Breaker Boys* is a work of fiction, I disguised the names of most Hazleton-area breakers and patch towns to give myself latitude about such logistical matters as their proximity to Hazleton and the dates of the strike. I kept the name Lattimer, however, because history was made there.

As for people, the only real names are those of union leader John Fahy (usually spelled Fahey in newspaper accounts of the time) and Luzerne County sheriff James Martin. And there *was* a boy named Connie—Cornelius Burke, age eleven—who came to the miners' aid after the shootings.

The Tanner family is fictional and is not intended to represent any one family of independent operators. In 1897, Lattimer and several other Hazleton collieries were owned by the Pardee family, my husband's ancestors. I myself am a descendant of Italian immigrants with names that include Raccio, Anastasia, Russo, and Cuticelli. All worked at menial jobs on railroads and in factories when they arrived in America. In *The Breaker Boys*, I have tried to balance the perspectives of both the operators and the immigrants.

GLOSSARY

NATE HEARS . . .	WHICH MEANS . . .	POLISH SPELLING
Brat	Brother	Brat
Chesh	Hi	Cześć
Chin-COO-yah	Thanks	Dziękuje
DOB-sheh	Good	Dobrze
Doe-veed-ZEN-yah	Goodbye	Do widzenia
DU-pa	Buttocks	Dupa
Go-WOMP-kee	Stuffed cabbage	Gołąbki
MAT-ka	Mother	Matka
Nyeh	No	Nie
OY-chets	Father	Ojciec
POL-ska	Poland	Polska
PONCH-kee	Doughnuts	Pączki
SHO-stra	Sister	Siostra
STO lat	Happy birthday (literally, "One hundred years!")	Sto lat
Tahk	Yes	Tak

In the story, Polish names are spelled the way Nate would have heard them as an English speaker, not necessarily with the proper Polish spelling.